I0593076

PROLOGUE

*T*he whistle of leather through the air barely gave time to react before the sting of the belt bit into his back. All William could do was curl in a ball and try to protect his head from the hard toe of his father's boots as he alternated between lashes and kicks.

"I told you, sissy boy, that I ain't wanting you playing them computer games. A real man hunts and works on cars, not sit in a room pretending to be elves and fairies. But you ain't shaping up to be a real man. Heck, at your age I could already hunt and dress deer carcasses without my pa. You can't even look at blood without vomiting." Contemptuously, he spat beside his prone son. At least while he was engrossed with his tirade the beating had stopped. "You're soft like your mama, and she left you. Ain't want nothing to do with a lily sissy boy like you. You hear me, boy? Your own mama didn't want you." Another brutal kick landed against his arms that were desperately shielding his face. William bit down against an agonized cry that tried to erupt, muffling it. *He might be a sissy, but he wasn't going to give his father the satisfaction of hearing him sob.* "Makes me think you ain't even mine."

1

Pain washed over William in great, white hot waves while he lay there listening to the heavy footsteps as his tormentor left the room. His throat was raw against unuttered protests and shouts as the click of the lock slid into place. Excruciatingly, he forced his abused body to unfurl from its position. Through the slits of his swelling eyes, he could see the ruined remains of his video console. He'd thought his father would be out for a few hours longer—enough time to clock the final level—but somehow time had gotten away from him, drawn into a world of fantasy where he was a hero, admired by all. Too late, he'd heard his father's angry voice behind him, a moment before the wrath of his fist.

The sobs he'd held in broke free, snot now mingling with the blood on his face as he agonizingly crawled over. Clutching the remains to his chest, hatred seethed for the brute who was his father. One day he'd leave this behind and never look back, just like the evil woman who'd left him there—his mother.

CHAPTER 1

*W*illiam would never understand, for as long as he lived, what had possessed Misty to uproot her life and leave civilization for Texas. If that wasn't bad enough, she'd invited him down to see her new ranch on the same weekend that a whiteout had hit New York City, forcing him into a completely unnecessary road trip. The fact he'd had to purchase a car to undertake said road trip spoke volumes about how he felt about driving even a short distance.

He didn't like to admit that it wasn't the same in New York since Misty had had the audacity to fall in love with that rodeo clown. Secretly, William harbored a liking for Logan. It took a special kind of man to know how to handle his business partner, and the cowboy had managed it and made her disgustingly happy to boot. It was just that now he was left feeling lonely and at loose ends in a city that never slept.

A loud knock from the engine pulled him back from his musing. William wasn't a mechanic—he barely knew one end of the car from the other, which his soft hands attested for—but the noise seemed at odds with the usual effortless purr the supercar had displayed on the trip so far. The navigation system teasingly showed that he was under twenty miles till he was at Misty's ranch and he could tell her exactly how much she owed him for the indignity she'd forced upon him.

The knock fell silent and William made a mental note to call the dealership when an almighty *kaboom* made him hit his head on the low ceiling. A cloud of black smoke trailed out from under the hood as the car ground to a halt. William pounded the palms of his hands against the wheel.

"You've got to be kidding me!"

Resigned, he pulled out his phone and began to search for the local mechanic, surprised that one shop had the same name as Misty's new beau—Erikson Mechanical Service. He knew there was a sister, but maybe Logan had a brother Misty had never mentioned. Rubbing a stinging palm on his trousers, he began to dial, praying a martini wasn't too far in his future or, at this rate, even a cold beer. He sniffed. *How the mighty have fallen.* And he hadn't even been in Texas for more than a couple of hours—imagine what he'd be like by the end of the week!

SHELBY WHISTLED, giving a double take as she took in the supercar pulled over by the side of the road. *What a beauty.* Parking the tow truck, she climbed out, eyes reverently glued to the perfection in front of her marveling eyes. Longingly, she ran a hand over its smooth, clean lines, half expecting it to disappear like some sort of mirage.

"Are you able to fix it?" a New York accent said behind her.

Shelby guiltily jerked her hand away, holding it behind

her back. "Well, sir, I haven't even seen what's under the hood," she said as she turned to address the car owner.

Blinking, her mouth dropped open. *Could it be? The man she'd spent way too much time fantasizing over was standing looking thoroughly fed up in front of her.* Shaking her head just to check it wasn't her mind playing tricks on her, she took a steadying breath. *Keep it together, Shelby, be cool.* Standing in the heat of the midday sun, she could tell he was a man who prided himself on his appearance—and why wouldn't he? His features were so perfect, even with moisture clinging to his brow, that somehow any more delicacy would have been too beautiful for a man. His black hair gleamed as the slight breeze ruffled it, his eyes—a tawny shade of brown—looked out at her from a face flushed with impatience and heat. *Remember, you're a professional, Shelby.* Lord, he even smelled good.

"If I could get you to do that now, I'll have a look."

Misty's business partner didn't seem to recognize her as he headed back to the driver's side. Not that that was much of a surprise. It wasn't as though someone like him would remember someone like her from a wedding. William—who Shelby was convinced was much more suited to Billy-muttered something.

"Sorry, what was that?" she asked.

"I said I can't do it."

"You don't know how to pop the bonnet?" *This wasn't how the fantasy usually played out in her head. By now he was usually stripped to the waist and asking her to hand him a spanner.*

"No, but I'm sure there's a manual for it. I'll just find it."

Shelby watched in surprise as he reached across to the glove compartment and withdrew a booklet. Wiping her brow, she wondered why he was driving a car like this if he didn't know every little detail about it. Heck, if it were hers, she'd probably sleep in it. With quick strides, she made her way to his side and located the button down near his seat, smiling in satisfaction as the hood finally opened. William flicked the manual crisply shut, his mouth thinning.

"Thank you." *Was he actually annoyed that she'd figured it out before him?*

Shelby made her way to the business end of the car. "You don't see many plug-in hybrids out this way. How does it compare to a regular car?"

"Not that good considering I'm on the side of the road with you."

Shelby laughed good-naturedly. "I reckon so. Well, that's something you don't see every day."

William peered at the engine. "What?"

"A twin turbo charged 3.0-liter V8." She pointed. "And look, not one, not two, but three electric motors as well. I read somewhere that it can go from zero to sixty-two miles per hour in two and a half seconds and, I mean, it's better for the environment, being a hybrid. What's the fastest you've ever gotten it to? I reckon it'd go faster than a sneeze through a screen door."

He blinked back at her. "I've done the speed limit."

What was wrong with the man? "Really? That's a waste."

"You seem to know a lot about my car."

She looked down at his manicured hands and then to her own, the nails encrusted with grease and grime and cut short. "It's my job to, and it's a gorgeous car that most people are lucky to see in the flesh in their lifetime. I'm going to back the tow truck and get it loaded."

He raised his brows, peering over his shades at her. "Can you fix it?"

"Possibly. Heck, I'd love the chance to try." Shelby's hands itched at the thought of the test drive afterwards. *To make sure it worked, of course.* "But only a dealer can get the genuine parts it needs. I can take it back to the garage and you can keep it there until you arrange transport back home."

"Thank you." William stood awkwardly, seemingly unsure of what to do next.

"I can give you a ride into town with your car." Heck, she'd take him clear to Mexico if that's what he wanted.

William gave a sharp nod. "I can have some friends come pick me up from there." As Shelby walked away, she pondered if she should be offended that he still had no idea who she was.

THE OVERNIGHT BAG looked as sorely out of place as he felt in a grease pit like this. Phone in hand, William watched from the office as the woman expertly lowered his car from the tow truck, several other mechanics coming over to admire it before pushing it back into a bay. Glancing around, he located a coffee pot and poured some into a Styrofoam cup, noting the stacks of paperwork on the desk and pinned to the wall behind it. *Seriously, it looks like they'd benefit from a good software package to streamline the business.* Judging from the ancient computer, it wasn't something they'd looked into. With a suspicious sniff of the dark brew, he tentatively sipped it, the AC rattling in the background. *At least I've finally stopped sweating.* He pulled his damp shirt away from his body, wrinkling his nose. William picked up a car magazine and disdainfully glanced down at the stained sofa in the office. No way was he risking his slacks on that disaster waiting to happen, it was bad enough that his shirt was ruined. He turned back to survey the rest of the workshop.

An assortment of cars in various stages of repair were in the bays, some on hoists and others either waiting to be worked on or for their owners to collect were parked in the lot outside. A strong smell of grease, gasoline and motor oil permeated the office, and dark smudges on the edge of the door clearly indicated that cleanliness was not a priority when entering.

Mouth thinning at the predicament he was in, William attempted another drink of coffee. Misty was going to have a field day with this when she heard about it. Curiously, he watched as the woman who had picked him up joked and jostled with the other mechanics. There was something about her, and he found himself wondering how she'd ended up getting stuck working on cars. She was taller than most women, a coltish look to her with sandy blonde hair that had ripples of strawberry when the sun hit it like it had out beside the highway. She always seemed to be smiling, her mouth a little too wide for her face, and her pale blue eyes sparkling like the water around the sun-kissed island he'd just bought—or at least from the brochure he'd seen of it. He was still mulling it over as she waved goodbye to her work-mates. William idly peered as each departed, wondering which one was Logan's brother, but none bore a resemblance. It didn't matter anyway. Frustration made him short-tempered. Clearly nothing more was going to be done today.

"Billy, your car's as snug as a bug in a rug tonight." The woman wiped her hands on a filthy rag.

"It's William." *Did he look like a Billy to her?* He needed to get the heck out of Texas if that were the case. *Maybe it didn't sound so bad in her slow molasses drawl.*

She barely blinked an eye at his correction. "Anyway, I can help arrange to get it back to the dealer for you, but I'm not sure how long that'll take. You're more than welcome to leave it here until that can be organized."

"Thank you. I'll give you the details of my PA, and she'll be able to liaise with you for the details."

"It may take a while. Most transporters are busier than a

hound with fleas this time of year. Can I give you a lift someplace?"

Unadulterated relief at the thought of leaving the grime behind washed the taste of the bad coffee from his mouth. "Do you know Misty Monroe?"

His companion regarded him with amusement. "We might've met once or twice."

"Do you know where she lives?"

"You have no idea who I am, do you?" There was a trace of laughter to her voice.

William peered closer at her. The color of her hair looked familiar, he just couldn't quite put his finger on it. "Ah?"

Her mirth finally escaped her in great peals. "You look as confused as a goat on AstroTurf. We met at Colt and Evelyn's wedding."

"I'm sorry, I don't remember meeting you." *Should I?*

"I was sitting right beside you, Billy. I'm Shelby Erikson, as in Logan Erikson's sister."

There was a certain irony that he'd just been saved by Logan's gorgeous sister. He'd never had a problem with capable women—his business partner was a prime example —but he felt decidedly off-balance at Shelby's revelation. *Yep, Misty was never going to let him forget about this.*

CHAPTER 2

ry as he might, even after Shelby had dropped him off at Misty's, he'd been unable to recall her from the wedding. *And she'd said she'd sat right beside him?* Misty had invited her back for dinner, and with a promise to head home real quick to clean up, the baffling mechanic had promptly driven away. Maybe when she was out of those overalls, his memory would be triggered. *Maybe in a dress.*

"What on earth possessed you to buy a car and drive here?" Misty handed him a mug of coffee. *Thank the Lord, civilization at last.*

"They canceled the flights and it was the only way."

Logan draped an arm around his girlfriend, shaking his head in amazement at William. "Most people don't go and buy a supercar for a road trip. Most normal people simply cancel."

William stiffened at the mocking look. "Answer me this, Logan. Would Misty have canceled?"

Misty pulled slightly away to gauge her boyfriend's reaction to the challenge. Obviously, she was as curious to hear the answer as William was. Logan threw his hands up in defeat. "Point made. Misty doesn't cancel anything, even when she should."

Misty put her hands on her hips. "Well, that's how things get done, Logan. William and I didn't become billionaires because we quit at the first hurdle."

"Exactly," agreed William. It was why they made such great business partners and friends. Misty understood how to get things done. "This lotus silk project isn't going to magically become a success if I curl up in defeat at every little thing. Speaking of defeats, I noticed you have a new car, Misty."

Logan cleared his throat awkwardly. "It's mine."

William's brows shot up. "Already letting the rich girl-friend buy you expensive toys?" He hadn't seen that one coming. It actually disappointed him a little.

"Behave yourself, William," warned Misty. "And I didn't buy it for him."

"Rodeo clowns must make more than I thought." William actually quite liked Logan, he just enjoyed riling the other man.

"Rodeo Protection Athlete," Logan corrected. William was convinced the other man did it more out of habit than offense. "And no, it pays as bad as you think. Colt gave it to me." Logan sheepishly looked at Misty. "For doing the auction."

His business partner raised her chin in defiance. "A deal's a deal." William had to give it to Misty, she'd always had a business mind. "Anyway, we're not talking about Logan's car, we're talking about yours. Heck, William, this is the first car you've ever owned. Even in college I had to drive you around in my old Volkswagen."

"Who's driving a Volkswagen?" Shelby asked, letting herself in. *Didn't people lock their doors in Texas?*

"Misty was telling us all about that car you have in your

workshop being William's first car." Logan grinned, clearly enjoying that morsel of news.

Shelby let out a low whistle. Disappointed, William noticed she wore old jeans, a vee neck T-shirt and baseball cap. Not a hint of makeup on her face. "Not bad for a first car. What did you drive when you got your license?"

Misty burst out laughing. William glared at her. "I borrowed the town car and got the driver to help me."

Shelby blinked. "Like, when you were a kid?"

"Like, when he was twenty-five." Misty roared with laughter, clutching at her sides. William thought it was a little overdone.

"Why did you wait till twenty-five? Didn't your pa show you? I was driving in the back paddock on my daddy's knee when I was five, and that was only because I couldn't reach the pedals."

Logan gave his kid sister a fond nudge with his shoulder. "And you were, like, ten when you pulled apart your first engine."

William stared at her in amazement. "Who let you pull a motor apart?"

Shelby shrugged. Clearly it was no big deal to her. "It was just from an old broken-down car that was in the barn when Dad and Mom bought the place. I put it back together when I was finished."

"What she didn't say is that she also got it working," Logan said proudly.

"But why did you do it in the first place?" William was beginning to feel like New York was a long way away.

"I wanted to figure out how it worked."

"Obviously." William regretted his tone when he saw the crushed look on Shelby's face. "When you say it like that, it seems obvious," he hastily amended, rewarded by her expression brightening. "Now, Misty, are you going to give me a tour of this ranch that pulled you away from New York?"

Misty happily linked arms with his. "I thought you'd never ask. Logan's much better at cooking the steaks than I am anyway, and it'll give you a chance to give me all the office gossip. Dana only tells me about the support staff." Relieved to finally be back on familiar territory, William allowed himself to be drawn from the room, leaving the siblings to stare at their departing backs.

It wasn't that Shelby meant to listen in on what Billy and Misty were talking about, it was just that they were speaking so passionately it was kind of hard not to.

"Did you see some of Mr Onissios's designs?" Shelby heard Misty ask.

"The silhouette he created is perfect for the drape of the lotus silk. It reminds me of a classic Chanel. Once it's launched, everyone who knows anything about fashion will know it belongs to the collection." Enthusiasm warmed Billy's voice.

"I've been in contact with the lotus farmers and informed them we need as much silk as they can produce. It's a stretch, and already I've extended interest free loans to several to extend their capabilities around staffing."

"I have figures around how many yards Mr Onissios will need. We can go over that whenever you'd like."

"Excuse me, ya'll," Shelby interrupted hesitantly, feeling like an intruder. "Logan has the steaks just the perfect side of medium rare. If ya'll don't hurry, he's liable to polish them all off himself."

"He wouldn't dare," Misty blustered, the gleam of battle flickering to life in her eyes. "Logan Erikson, you get your hands off the steak," she called as she hurried to protect her meal.

"For what it's worth, I don't think Logan would actually eat them all," Shelby said, giving a half smile to Billy. *Lord, he's one gorgeous man. Just act cool, Shelby.*

"I can imagine he won't if he knows what's good for him. Misty will make sure of it."

Shelby laughed. "She'd probably raise hell and stick a chunk under it."

Billy grimaced in good humor. "I guess you could say that." He gestured for her to precede him. "Shall we go get our meals before they're taken as spoils of war?"

"I reckon." A happy glow flowed through her as she brushed past him. He was such a gentleman. *Might even teach some of these fellas out here a thing or two.* "How long are you here for?"

"Only a few days. At least I don't have to go through the horror of that drive again."

How anyone driving a car like that down the highway could consider it in such unflattering terms was beyond Shelby. "Oh, so you've booked a flight?"

If the look Billy directed at her was ever so slightly patronizing, she chose to ignore it as they made their way to the dining room. "No, I arranged for Misty's plane to collect me."

Feeling foolish to think a billionaire traveled on commercial airlines, she buttoned her mouth shut, relieved when they rejoined the others. Shelby ignored the little knot of self-doubt that settled in her belly at the thought of appearing not sophisticated enough for Billy. Shaking it loose, she decided she was what she was, and he might as well start getting used to it now because she wasn't changing anytime soon.

SHELBY SWUNG the pink rope experimentally in her hand, admiring the way it sliced through the air. Beneath her, the chestnut mare's ears twitched back and forth, nostrils flared as she focused on the calf in the box. Her pulse beginning to race, she pressed her hat down firmly in place. Poppy sprung forward early only to stop when the horse realized that the calf hadn't escaped the box for her to chase.

"Steady, gal," Shelby murmured. Her body began to tense, the chatter of the announcer fading into the background, and then the calf exploded out into the arena, Poppy erupting after it, breaking the barrier.

The rope whistled in the air, one swing, two, and then released, seeking the calf like a laser-guided missile. Shelby sat deep in the saddle, Poppy's haunches bunching as she slid to a halt, and the string at the end of the rope snapping free from the saddle horn. Satisfaction at having done a good job filled her. Not half because in the stands, against his loud protests at being forced to go to a rodeo, sat Billy.

"You did a good job." Logan handed her rope back to her as she made her way out of the arena. "Enough to be in the money at least."

"Any day I leave the arena having roped the calf and still on the horse is a good day," Shelby said humbly. She rodeoed because she liked the comradery and the thrill it gave her. She was perfectly content knowing she was only good enough to do the local circuit. Heck, not everyone was going to be a champion. Didn't mean she didn't love doing it.

"I feel the same about not ending up on the end of horns." Logan laughed. "Now I need to get back out there."

Shelby watched her brother jog back toward the arena, brightly colored scarves swinging with each bouncy stride he took. Chuckling to herself, she headed back to her trailer, waving at Colt as he warmed up his horse, Big Wheels, for the next event. She gave her mare a pat. "There's your big brother."

She'd never forget the day Colt and Logan had turned up with the orphaned foal in the back seat of Colt's pickup. Poppy's mom had died, and the little chestnut filly had needed around-the-clock care. Shelby had lost count of all the bottles she'd made, or nights spent in the stable. Heck, she'd even had a little pen made at the mechanics workshop so she could be the best horse-mommy she could be. Poppy was her heart horse. There would never be another after her.

Giving the mare's gleaming coat a final pat, Shelby swung her tack into the back of her truck. Poppy didn't even bother raising her head from the hay bag. *Such a greedy guts.* She smiled fondly at her horse. Making sure her mint green shirt was free of horsehair and tucked in, she went in search of food … and Billy.

Some people liked to go from food truck to food truck seeing what was new, but this wasn't Shelby's first rodeo. She knew what was good. A couple of stops and she was loaded up with food and a frozen strawberry margarita and was on her way to the stands. Spying her friends, she made her way over, winking at Hope between Evelyn and Misty and taking a seat beside Billy.

"Not much longer and Hope will be old enough to compete," she said, setting her drink on the bleacher beside her.

"Not you, too," groaned Evelyn. "I had to talk Colt out of loading Freckles in the trailer."

"Ride poddies," the little girl solemnly announced.

"Well, her grandmother rode bulls back in the day. Maybe Hope will, too." Shelby took a bite of her fried Thanksgiving dinner ball. It was almost better than her mom's.

"Suddenly having her be led around the barrels doesn't seem so bad," Evelyn said.

"Logan and Colt wouldn't let anything happen to her, and it's not like the poddies are that big. I did it when I was only a little older than her."

"Your parents put you on cows when you were little?" Billy was aghast. "Didn't they love you?"

Shelby took a sip of her drink, the icy strawberry cooling. "Of course they love me. I mean, you've met me. I'm incredibly lovable. But it's no big deal. We're raised tough in Texas, and it's poddy calves, not cows. You don't come to rodeos much, do you?"

"No, I'm more of a grand prix racing and polo man."

Billy seemed to be eyeing off what she was eating. Realizing she'd forgotten her manners, she held out her plate to him. "Want one?"

"I'm not even sure what you're eating."

"Well, this one"—she pointed to the half-eaten ball—"is a deep-fried Thanksgiving dinner ball, and it's got turkey, stuffing and corn all battered and fried and comes with this cranberry sauce and gravy to dip it in. And this"—she pointed to the other plate she had stacked on top—"is a personal favorite. It's deep-fried milk and cookies." She leaned in closer. "But it's not really. It's just Oreo ice-cream, battered and fried."

"I don't think I've ever had one."

"You should try one. Broaden your horizons, William," Misty encouraged, watching the exchange with an amused gaze.

"When in Rome, I guess." Billy reached over and took the milk and cookie ball, bringing it to his mouth.

Inspiration struck Shelby. "Hang on, Billy." She grabbed his phone and, before he could react with the treat frozen halfway to his mouth, took a selfie of them both. "Now you have proof you tried it." Stunned, Billy blinked before taking a tentative bite. "You don't have to say it. It's good, right? You look happier than a clam at high tide."

Billy wiped his mouth with a napkin Misty handed him. "It's not as bad as I thought it'd be," he admitted, surprising Shelby by taking another bite. "It grows on you."

Shelby sure as heck hoped she was growing on him too.

CHAPTER 3

"*Y*ou see the way the fabric drapes?" Mr Onissios peered from where he stood with his arm outstretched, the lotus silk hanging from it. "It is amazing, the way it breathes and moves."

William leaned forward to rub the fabric between his fingers, caught in the designer's passion. "Once this collection hits, a lot of other designers are going to want to work with it."

Cunningness gleamed from Mr Onissios's narrowed eyes. "I would expect that I would have first access to what lotus silk I require."

"For this collection, yes." The thrill of holding the power in the negotiation made William smile blandly. "However, with the scarcity of this textile, it will come at a premium after this."

"The rarer the gem, the more valuable it is," the designer agreed, no doubt already hearing the ring of cash registers.

"Speaking of that, from this shipment of lotus silk I would like a suit made. I think something like this."

William opened the photos on his phone to find where

he'd saved it, the designer looking over his shoulder. The selfie Shelby had taken at the rodeo stared up at him. Midway ready to swipe to the next one, he paused. There he was, expression horrified, fried ball halfway to his open mouth. Embarrassment flushed hot through him *I should've deleted this as soon as she'd taken it.* He didn't know why he hadn't. Shelby, well, she looked completely at home. The way her pretty strawberry blonde hair hung out from beneath her cowboy hat, her pale blue eyes laughing as she grinned.

"Is this your girlfriend?"

William laughed at the suggestion, too startled to deny it straightaway. "That's Shelby. If I'm very much not mistaken, and I rarely am, she's soon to be Misty's sister-in-law."

"Not your girlfriend?" *Why was it so important to Mr Onissios if Shelby was single or not?* He didn't really take Shelby as his type.

"No, she's not my girlfriend."

"What agency is she with?" persisted the designer.

William laughed, trying to disguise his irritation at the continued questioning. To be fair, the idea of Shelby as part of the fashion world was amusing. She was too genuine, too real. "She's not."

"She should be. Look at that bone structure. Her look is unique." Mr Onissios waved his arms dramatically in the air. "I have had inspiration. I want her as the face of this collection."

"I don't think that's going to happen." William never agreed to anything he couldn't deliver. Turning Logan's sister into a high-fashion model? Well, he had more chance of scoring the winning touchdown at the Super Bowl.

The designer folded his arms across his chest, staring William down. "Make it happen. If I don't have my muse for this collection, there won't be one."

William sighed. *And it had all been going so well...*

❧

"HELLO, ERIKSON MECHANICS, SHELBY HERE." Shelby balanced the phone against her shoulder as she wiped her hands clean on a rag.

"Hello, Shelby. It's William."

She went slack in shock at hearing his voice on the other end of the phone, the receiver sliding off her shoulder and toppling to the floor. "Oh shoot," she cried, frantically clutching at it. Breathlessly, she brought it back to her ear. "Are you still there, Billy?"

"Yes, we seem to have a bad line. It sounds like there's a bit of static."

"Yeah, the static's bad," she agreed. "Look, I know what you're calling about."

"You do?" he seemed surprised.

"Yeah, your car got put on the transport yesterday afternoon. I spoke to that nice lady, Dana, and she said she'd make sure you got the message. I reckon the dealership should be giving you a call any day now."

"Thank you, Dana sent me an email about it. However, that's not what I'm calling you about."

Shelby nearly dropped the phone again. "Oh." Her heart beat faster at the prospect that his call wasn't for business, but for pleasure. Maybe he liked her, too.

"I have a way that you don't have to run that old mechanic shop anymore. Improve your situation in life."

The happiness gushed from her body like a deflating balloon. "I like my situation in life, and ever since I was a little gal, all I wanted was to work on cars and own my own garage." *Didn't he think she was good enough, working as a mechanic?*

"But you can do better," Billy insisted.

"You must think I'm dumb as a box of rocks, but I'm

doing exactly what I want to be doing. So, you go peddle your produce somewhere else cause, Billy, I ain't interested." Shelby, breathless with rage and not a small dose of hurt, slammed the phone down, hanging up on him. *What a jerk!* She wasn't going to waste any more time dreaming about him, that's for sure.

～

"DANA SAID you wanted me to call you. You do know I got all of your messages, right?" Misty sounded exasperated on the other end of the line. "I was out."

"Shopping?" William couldn't imagine there were any luxury shops like Misty was used to for miles around the ranch.

"No, *out*. As in, outside. I was helping Logan feed up the stock."

William shuddered at the thought of all the dirt and smells that would have been involved with that particular enterprise. "Sounds farmy. I need to discuss Mr Onissios's latest demand."

"Really? I thought we had it all locked in."

"He has one more. He wants Shelby to be the face of the collection. He declared her as his muse."

"How does he even know who Shelby is?"

"He saw a picture of her on my phone." William still couldn't believe he hadn't deleted that picture from the rodeo. Actually, he didn't even know why he'd let himself get talked into going to it in the first place.

"Why was there a picture of Shelby on your phone? Is there anything you want to tell me?" Misty teased.

William rolled his eyes. Yeah, she was always going to pick up on that little morsel. "It was one she took at that rodeo. Now focus, Misty, the issue is that he says if he doesn't have Shelby as his muse, he won't do the collection."

"Well, that's not a problem. I'm sure Shelby will do anything you ask her."

William sighed, closing his eyes at his business partner's words. *Why was she making this so difficult?* "You're wrong. I just tried, and she hung up on me."

"What on earth did you say to her?" demanded Misty.

"Nothing. I just explained that she wouldn't have to live like she is now if she does it," he replied in a defiant rush of words.

"Oh, William. Why would you say it like that?"

"What do you mean? I thought she'd jump at the opportunity I was offering." *Why was she acting like he was the bad guy?*

Misty gave a long-suffering sigh. "You wouldn't understand. Look, I'll talk to her and see if I can try to fix it, but I'm not promising anything. Oh, and William?"

"Yes?"

"Maybe don't talk to Shelby about how she lives her life again."

William hung up, mystified at why he was the villain in the story now. *Obviously, there was something wrong with Shelby. What normal person didn't want wealth and fame? Who actually wanted to live in a small town, getting dirty every day?* William shuddered. Certainly not him.

CHAPTER 4

Shelby was on the extreme ends of her toes, every fiber in her body stretched to its limits trying to get the wrench on the nut. She'd tried getting at it from underneath, but the angle had been all wrong. "Hi, Shelby."

Startled, she jerked, hitting her head on the engine block she'd been wedged against. "Son of a gun!" Extracting herself out from under the hood, she gave Misty a baleful glare as she rubbed her throbbing temple. "Don't go sneaking up on me. You know I have the reactions of a ninja cat."

"Sorry," Misty apologized cheerfully. "I thought you saw me pull up."

"How the heck was I meant to do that while hanging nearly upside down, the only thing keeping me anchored being my pinky toe?" Shelby reached for her bottle of water and held it against her head, hoping it would stop the ache.

"So, I heard William gave you a call." Misty gave her a sideways glance.

"If you want to call it that. Thank the stars I won't have to hear from him ever again now that his car is out of my work-shop and out of my hair." Nothing left a bitter taste in the mouth like someone not living up to the fantasy, and Shelby had built a rather nice one around the New York dandy. "Even taking Poppy for a long ride didn't make up for having to hear from that jerk."

"What did he actually tell you about it?" Misty hedged.

"That I would be taken away from this miserable hovel and live like some sort of Cinderella." The bottle crackled under her ferocious grip. "Silly me, didn't know I needed rescuing."

"William can sometimes be a little tactless about things like that. I take it it didn't go down well?"

"About as well as a cup of cold vomit."

Misty winced, scrunching her face up in disgust. "Wow, that's a visual I didn't need. But did he actually tell you what it was all about?"

"No." And as far as she was concerned, she didn't need to know.

"Okay, how about we both sit down and I'll tell you a little bit about it, and if you still don't want anything to do with it, I understand." Misty indicated two old camp chairs against the wall, and after a moment's hesitation, Shelby headed over. "I'm on a board for a charity that helps fund women getting into business in Third World and developing countries. I mainly provide funds and, where possible, expertise, such as a website or such. Now, the really exciting thing I've been hearing about is this lotus silk. It's a really amazing eco-friendly microfiber they get from lotus stems and it's all done by hand. And I mean literally every single step from gathering to spinning through to weaving. It's time intensive. The end result is a fabric that is like a cross between silk and linen. Now, William and I think, with our contacts, we can create a demand for it as a luxury textile. We have a world-renowned fashion designer, Mr Onissios from the fashion house Oni, who has agreed to do a collection featuring lotus silk." Misty paused to draw breath.

"That's fascinating, but I don't understand what this has to do with me." *Or Billy calling me.* Shelby found herself drawn in by the passion in Misty's voice. Absentmindedly, she patted the chicken that had settled herself on her lap.

"Mr Onissios wants you to be the face of the collection."

"How does he even know who I am?"

"Because he saw your picture on William's phone."

Shelby sat thunderstruck, staring at Misty. *Billy had a photo of her on his phone?* He must have kept the selfie from the rodeo! Her heart sang with delight. "I'm flattered, I think, but I don't want anything to do with modeling. It would be like the mean gals from high school all over again." She shuddered at the memory. "No, thanks. I'm much happier working with the guys at the workshop."

Misty peered at her, a speculative gleam in her worldly eyes. "Do you have a passport?"

"Yeah, from that holiday we went to in Mexico." She wasn't sure she was pleased with this change in conversation. "Why?"

"Good." Misty stood as if something had been settled. As far as Shelby could tell, they hadn't agreed to anything. At least, she didn't think so? "There are some people you need to meet. People who are relying on you doing this.

"Why are they relying on me?" Shelby rose, conscious that she didn't want to look up at Misty. "They don't even know me."

"Mr Onissios has said that he will only do the collection if you are the face. In fact, he started calling you his muse. No you, no collection, no helping the lotus silk women." Satisfied she'd sufficiently guilted Shelby, she brushed her clothing off. "It's time for a little trip."

"Who's going to feed Poppy and my chickens? Not to

mention the worms." Shelby thought she was saying no, but she couldn't be sure with how Misty was acting.

"I'm sure I can prevail upon Logan to take care of the animals."

"I have a business to run." *That ought to put a stop it.*

"I'm sure I can arrange someone to run the office, and the other mechanics can cover for you. I'll pay them twice their weekly wages if it will help." Misty stared challengingly back at her.

In a last-ditch effort, Shelby wailed. "I don't really have time for a trip."

Misty smiled smugly at her. "Funny, William said the same thing."

ONE OF THE perks of being disgustingly rich was that one could do whatever the heck they felt like, whenever they felt like it. Business commitments aside, of course. It had afforded William the opportunity to travel extensively, but until this moment, he'd never set foot in Myanmar, formerly known as Burma. Along with Vietnam and Cambodia, it was one of the countries that would be supplying the lotus silk for their little foray into the fashion world.

From the comfort of his plush leather chair, he cast a sideways glance at where Shelby was seated beside Misty, staring out the window at the clouds floating past her window. William wasn't sure what his business partner had said to the cowgirl, but it had been enough to get her to set foot on the plane. He might have moaned dramatically about being dragged along on this little adventure, but secretly, he was excited to discover a new place.

"This is your captain speaking. The crew will be

preparing the cabin for landing," a familiar voice sounded over the intercom.

William turned to stare at Misty in surprise. "Isn't that Captain Wilson's voice? The helicopter pilot?"

"Yeah, the regular pilot is on holidays, and Captain Wilson offered to step in. It's okay, I believe he does know how to fly a plane as well." Misty didn't even bother looking up from her magazine. William was bemused to see a tractor on its cover. "Now, I suggest we do what he says and get ready to land. I have my contact for the small business funding project meeting us at the airport. She's going to take us out to see several of the farms that grow the lotus, and then to the workshops that turn the stalks into the most wonderous fiber."

William settled back in his seat, wondering what Shelby was going to make of this experience. She didn't appear to be a worldly traveler. Honestly, he'd been surprised that she'd owned a current passport. She had, for her part, appeared to have moved on from her pique at him.

"Have you met any of them before?" Shelby asked, eyes shining brightly. She looked like a kid getting ready to see her birthday cake. *I guess that answers the question, then.*

"I've met Myitzu via computer hook-up, but not in person, and none of the others that we'll meet today. It's very hard to get in touch remotely in some of the areas. Only twenty-six percent of the population have access to electricity and that's obviously mostly around the capital city. Where we're going is more rural."

"Will it take us long to get there?" Shelby seemed fascinated. "I don't really know much about Myanmar. How did you get involved with the country?"

"Not too long. The entire country is a little smaller than Texas." Misty seemed to be warming to her subject. "I got involved being part of a project that provides interest free loans to women who have or want to start a small business. Per capita, the income is roughly seven hundred dollars, and there are a lot of issues around women's rights. Sexual violence, trafficking and discrimination are common experiences for girls and women here. The governments are working hard to fix that. They've also set targets to reduce poverty, and it appears to be working with reforms in their economy and outside assistance from the likes of our program."

Shelby's mouth turned down sadly. "At least they're fixin' things, I guess."

William felt his stomach lurch as they began their descent. "They have a complicated history that hasn't helped. They went from being occupied by the British until 1948, and then it gained its independence to be under military rule for another fifty years."

"That's true," Misty agreed. "But the people are wonderfully warm and friendly—or at least the ones I've met remotely are—and so interesting. There are at least one hundred and thirty-five different ethnic groups all with their own identities, cultures, customs, histories and, in most cases, language. It's a fascinating country."

Waiting for the ladies to make their way to the hatch first, William shielded his eyes as he slid his sunglasses into place in defense against the bright light bombarding him. He noted wryly that Misty was already embracing the small dark-haired woman who waited for them on the tarmac, Shelby quickly following suit.

"Myitzu, this is William, who I'm sure I've spoken of. He has been a key part of getting this venture off the ground."

He found himself on the end of a friendly open gaze. He quickly held his hand out to fend off the potential hug that may have been coming his way. "It's a pleasure to meet you. I've heard a great deal about your lotus silk."

"And I have heard just as much about your business skill and sense of fashion. It fills all of us with great belief that you have chosen to help us." Myitzu gestured to the car waiting for them. "If you would like, we can go to the fields now."

"I can't wait." Shelby bounced a little in her boots. *It was actually kind of adorable how excited she was.*

William looked out his window at the cityscape flashing past his car window as they made their way down the busy tree-lined streets. The architecture made him feel like he'd stepped back in time to a bygone era. The structures had the look of colonial government buildings with stately columns and cream façades. But now most appeared to be in a state of disarray.

"What happened here? The buildings look so sad." Shelby had obviously noticed the same.

"This used to be the capital of Burma. Some of these buildings were government, some owned by wealthy citizens from all over the world when it was a thriving colonial city. But several years ago when we were still under military rule, it was decided to create a new capital city. So they did, and now no one maintains these buildings. It is our hope that they will be restored back to their former glory." Myitzu spoke hopefully.

"It would be a shame not to preserve it," agreed Misty. William swore he could already hear the cogs turning in her head. *I wonder how Logan will like spending time here.*

"Is it normal for the men to wear skirts?" Shelby asked in astonishment. "I don't mean to be rude, but I don't think I've seen a man wearing pants yet."

Myitzu smiled at the other woman's words. "It's called a longyi, and both men and women wear it."

"Billy, how about we get you in one before we leave? Maybe we could send some pictures to the designer for ideas." Shelby made a show of looking him up and down.

William laughed at her cheeky comment. "I'm not the one who's his muse. I wouldn't want to steal the crown from you."

"You make it sound as welcome as a porcupine at a nudist colony, but I think you'd love to steal it." Misty chuckled at Shelby's saucy reply, quickly explaining in plainer English to the Myanmar woman what had just been said.

"Why do I feel like I should be writing down all your colloquialisms?" *There was something about the way she could turn a phrase that rolled off the tongue.* Sure, it wasn't something you'd want to hear on Park Avenue, but it was still amusing nonetheless.

"You know where to find me if you want to take notes. And Billy, I won't even charge you for the privilege." William chuckled, shaking his head. He couldn't remember the last time he'd met someone as refreshingly unique as Shelby.

For the rest of the day as they met women and children, he was struck by how natural Shelby was with her interactions with them. When a child would offer up a flower or some other treasure, she would exclaim in delight, making a fuss as though they'd shown her the crown jewels. William didn't quite understand it at all. From where he stood, it was just a rock or weed, but it seemed to win them over, the women giving her shy smiles and the children following on her heels like puppies.

At one point, one of the women had whispered to Myitzu, pointing at him and Shelby. When it had been translated to Misty, she'd burst out in a gale of laughter. No amount of pleading had been able to get her to share the source of her mirth, but William had a sneaking suspicion it was him.

After a surprisingly good meal at the hotel, Shelby excused herself to head upstairs to call her parents. Apparently, they were looking after some ducks or something of hers.

"You know she has a crush on you, right?" Misty eyed him speculatively over the rim of her champagne glass.

"I think Shelby's just being friendly." The thought was flattering, but they were two very different people.

"She is friendly, I'll give her that, but it's more than that. Look, William, I love you to bits and you're my best friend, but Shelby's too good for you."

The sting of betrayal turned the cognac sour in his mouth as he spluttered on normally delicious liquor. "What do you mean?" Finally clearing his throat, he glared his offense at her.

"What you see is what you get with Shelby. There's no artifice, no guile. She's got a pure heart and believes the best in people." Misty dismissively fluttered her hands at him. "You, on the other hand, are jaded, cynical and grouchy, and don't even get me started on the façade you hide behind. Remember, I knew you before you became The William Irvine."

"It's a good thing I'm not interested."

"Keep it that way."

William didn't know why her words, complete with a mildly threatening tone, made him feel like he'd just agreed to something he didn't want to. Returning to his drink, hopeful that this time it wouldn't turn on him, he put the odd sensation up to jet lag. Nothing the fine cognac wouldn't be able to cure.

CHAPTER 5

*H*umiliation scalded Shelby's cheeks as she read the message that flashed up on her phone. "Son of a gun," she swore. Quickly, she dialed her brother's number.

"That was quick. I think you might've broken some sort of record there."

She gritted her teeth at her brother's jovial mood. "What do you mean you heard I had a crush and he wasn't even Texan?"

"That you have a crush and he isn't even Texan," Logan drawled back.

"Who says I have a crush on anyone?"

"Misty does, and it's not just on anyone. It's on your Billy."

"He's not my Billy!" *Not that she hadn't fantasized about what that would feel like.*

"Well, obviously. He's too pretty for you."

"He's not pretty. He's handsome and cares about how he looks."

"And you're still sticking with you don't have a crush on him?"

"ARGH!" Frustrated, Shelby hung up the phone. Misty better have a good explanation for why she was telling her brother she had crushes on people. Conveniently, the object of her displeasure's room was adjacent to her own. Flinging the door open, she stomped the several yards and knocked.

"Come in, it's open," Misty called from inside.

Throwing the door open, Shelby stormed in, glaring at Misty standing near the window. "What's the deal with telling Logan I have a crush on Billy? Heck, I don't even know if I like him like that yet." Who was she kidding? Of course she did. But still, Misty didn't need to go blabbing it around.

"Interesting," an amused male voice said from her left. Too late, Shelby spied Billy in the armchair with its back to her.

She flushed miserably. Knowing there was no way she could salvage the situation and that she wasn't sticking around to hear more, she spun on her heels and fled.

"Shelby, come back," Misty called after her. "William, did you really have to say something?"

Shelby slammed the door shut behind her and escaped to her room, not wanting to hear his reply. Hot, mortified tears filled her eyes. *He must think I'm such an idiot.*

"Is it okay if I come in?" Misty asked quietly. "You didn't lock the door."

Shelby scrubbed at her face. "Yeah."

"I'm sorry, I didn't mean to upset you. I sure as heck didn't expect Logan to say anything to you."

Shelby sniffed. "I know you didn't. Billy must think I've fallen off the turnip truck after what I just said."

Misty handed her a tissue. "For what it's worth, I've already told William not to get any ideas about you."

She blew her nose. "Really?"

"Really. I told him you were way too good for him."

"Oh, but I'm not. At least, I don't want to be." Warmth flooded Shelby's cheeks as she realized what she'd just admitted.

Misty gave her a sympathetic smile and squeezed her hand. "Don't sell yourself short. And well, William is William. He dates but he never gets serious, and he's had a lot of different girlfriends over the years. Sometimes I think he loses interest before he's even finished the first date."

"Maybe he just hasn't met the right gal to hold his attention." A glimmer of hope flared to life. *Maybe he was tired of all the beautiful, empty people and needed someone more down to earth … like her!*

"Maybe. Now wash your face. We have one more visit this afternoon and it's one I really want you to see."

"I don't think I can face Billy." Shelby felt sick at the thought.

"You can, and I'm sure William has already forgotten it." Shelby knew Misty was trying to be reassuring, but it stung a little that Billy might have already moved on from it. Sighing, she headed to the bathroom. *Better get it over and done with.*

MISTY HAD PULLED out all the stops for this last visit. The jewel in her Myanmar crown—a visit to a thriving lotus plantation and silk factory. Although factory wasn't really the right word for it, William decided. There was no machinery, for one. Instead women with yellow painted on their faces gathered the flowers from the water and delivered them to a timber building, the sides open to allow for airflow in the heat of the afternoon. Inside more women were gathered at wooden benches, pulling the stems apart to reveal several thin strands of fiber and deftly rolled them together to create a yarn. At the back, several looms clacked and clattered as the shaft was passed back and forth, and slowly, inch by painstaking inch, fabric was created. It was an old-world kind of magic, one of patience and skill. Maybe Misty had a right to be proud. It was, after all, the very first venture she'd given an interest free loan to and it also happened to be Myitzu's.

With a flourish, the small women presented them with lotus silk scarves. William could only marvel at what had once been the innards of a plant stem now wondrously soft and pliable.

Shelby held hers to her cheek. "Thank you, Myitzu. I've never felt anything so soft."

"I would hope so, for a four-hundred-dollar scarf," William couldn't resist saying.

Swiftly, she pulled it away from her face. "I feel like I should've washed my hands or something before I touched it."

Myitzu laughed. "Lotus silk should be touched and admired. We hope that when people see you wearing it, Shelby, they will want to buy."

A worried light in her eyes cast shadows over Shelby's face. "I hope I don't let you down."

The small woman touched the tall cowgirl's hand gently. "You won't. You are the perfect person to represent us. Tall, strong, but with a fragile, delicate core from which something wonderous is created."

William wasn't sure why Myitzu finished her statement with a quick glance in his direction. It wasn't like she was comparing him to the most expensive fabric in the world. He wondered if Misty had told her about the scene back at the hotel earlier.

Later as he sat in the hotel lobby waiting for Shelby and

Misty to appear for dinner, he found himself stroking the luxurious fabric and thinking about the Texan cowgirl. Shelby was different to most of the women he'd ever met. With Misty as the only exception, there weren't many women he'd given more than a fleeting thought to for longer than a day. Somehow Shelby had continued to worm her way into his consciousness.

As if his thoughts had materialized into solid flesh, Shelby appeared, making her way over to him. She was wearing a softly flowing maxi dress in a vivid turquoise and black print that set her tan off to perfection. William was pretty sure her glorious light blue eyes would be glowing as well. As she came closer, he saw, to his satisfaction, they were.

"Oh, Misty isn't here yet?" She nibbled on her bottom lip, awkwardly looking around.

William stood and solicitously gestured to the wicker armchair beside him. "I'm sure she won't be too much longer. Can I get you something to drink?"

She settled into the deep cushions. "A glass of water would be great. My mouth's drier than a popcorn fart."

He blinked at the vision she had so succinctly presented him with. "In that case, waiter!" He snapped his fingers to garner attention. "This young lady is in need of refreshment urgently."

Shelby giggled the most marvelous sound of mirth. Light and genuinely filled with joy. "Billy, stop being so dramatic."

"If a popcorn fart isn't something to be dramatic about, I don't know what is."

"Excuse me." A concierge appeared in front of them. "Miss Monroe has asked me to give her apologies. She has a migraine and will not be able to attend dinner tonight."

"Oh." Alarmed, Shelby looked at him. "I hope she's all right. Maybe I should stay and look after her." She shifted in her chair, tugging at her dress. William thought she looked uneasy without her denim to hide behind.

"She said you might say that and asked me to reassure you that she's taken some medication and the best thing is for her to stay in a quiet, dark room. She asks that you and Mr Irvine go out and enjoy this last night in our beautiful city." There was a soothing cadence to the way the man spoke, gentle as the sea lapping at the shore.

"I don't know." Shelby cast her gaze about, looking at anything except him. It dawned on William that she would prefer to eat alone in her room rather than with him, such was her embarrassment over the earlier incident.

"Would you like to have dinner with me, Shelby? We haven't seen anything except for Misty's planned itinerary. Maybe, after we eat, we could go and explore." William gave her his best puppy dog eyes that had never failed him before —not that he'd ever had to employ them that often.

"I would like to see the sights." Shelby's voice was hesitant, still not willing to commit.

William turned to the concierge, deciding to take the matter in hand. *Clearly, Shelby needed a little nudge in the right direction.* "Thank you for letting us know. If Miss Monroe asks, please let her know that we've decided to dine out as originally planned." The man gave a sharp nod, his hair darkly gleaming under the lights, and backed away. "Now, Shelby, don't stand me up." He rose and held his hand out to her.

Looking down at her sandal clad feet, she pursed her lips before sighing in defeat. "My mom didn't raise me to be rude." Unfolding her legs, she stood. Together they walked from the serene hotel foyer and out into the night beyond.

"Would you like to eat first or go explore?" he asked above the traffic noise.

She turned shining eyes to him. "I'd really like to explore."

"Your wish is my command." William gave a little flourish as he bowed, setting Shelby to giggling. *Good, she was starting to relax*. He might as well address the elephant in the room. "For what it's worth, Misty told me her little theory too."

Shelby's eyes went from shining with excitement to stunned horror in a matter of second. "No," she breathed.

"And I told her that I don't think you have a crush on me. And then I heard it from your own mouth that you don't like me." William still wasn't sure what the sting he'd felt at her words had meant. More than likely wounded pride and nothing more. "So that's that."

"I mean, it's not that I don't like you, but I don't like like you." Shelby stumbled over her words.

"It's okay, I got what you meant." Deciding it had been discussed enough, he pointed to a tree, its buttressed roots flaring out at its base, a perfect counterpart to its limbs stretching into the inky sky above. People gathered around it and poured the contents of little clay pots on the ground beneath it before wandering away again. "What do you think they're doing?"

"That's a banyan tree, and they're making offerings to it." Shelby's tone was precisely matter of fact, as if it should be obvious. Honestly, William was a little taken aback that she'd known the answer. He'd actually asked it because he was planning on suggesting they go over and find out more. His surprise must have shown on his face since she started giggling. "Myitzu told me today when I saw one."

"Did you happen to ask her why some of the men have red teeth?" he asked as they continued to stroll down the street.

"I did."

"Well, don't keep me in suspense." The tantalizing smell of food cooking began to make his stomach grumble.

"It has to do with the betel nut they chew. Kinda like

chewing tobacco back home, I guess. What is that amazing smell?" Shelby stood on her tiptoes, trying to find the source.

"I think it's coming from that vendor over there." William pointed further down the street.

Shelby grabbed his hand and began to tow him along. "I'm getting some."

He was acutely aware of the touch of her hand in his and almost stumbled over a piece of uneven pavement, snapping him back to the world around him. "Are you sure? Don't you think the restaurant we're booked into would be a better option?"

She simply tugged on his hand again, not slowing her pace. "Come on, Billy, live a little. You'd never had deep-fried Thanksgiving dinner balls before and you loved them."

He had to give that to her. Maybe she was right. Maybe it was time to undo the proverbial top button and loosen up a bit. Giving a shrug, he followed the cowgirl.

"Can I have one?" Shelby held up her index finger to the man.

"Shouldn't you ask what it is first?" William peered at the various chopped and prepared ingredients.

Shelby scrunched her face up at him. "Why?"

"So, you know what you're eating." He stared at her. *Surely, the why was obvious.*

"No. I'm going to eat it and decide if I like it solely on what it tastes like."

"Sounds risky."

Shelby rolled her eyes at him. "Live like you mean it, Billy, not like it's a practice run."

"Fine. Make it two."

He had to blink at the brilliance of her smile. Like he'd done something amazing and she was proud of him. Turning back to the street vendor, she held up two fingers. "Two, please."

Surprisingly, it wasn't too bad. Some sort of noodle and curry, possibly chicken, with egg and salad. They continued their walk as they ate before standing in front of a glorious pagoda. Lights lit it up, its steep shimmering roof appearing liquid as it glinted and reflected it surroundings. It was like the ancient heart of the city, still proudly beating.

"It's beautiful," Shelby breathed. "I never knew something like that existed. How old do you think it is?"

"What, Myitzu didn't tell you?" he couldn't resist teasing. "I don't know, maybe a couple of thousand years old."

"You know, Misty kinda made me come on this trip."

"Me too."

She gave him a wry smile at his words. "And I'm glad she did. These people are so nice and friendly. They're good folk. If me getting all dolled up will help them prosper, then I need to do it."

"Does that mean Shelby Erikson is going to be a model?"

"I don't know if I could ever be a model, but I'll wear that fancy designer's clothes that he makes and smile at the camera." She stopped staring at him, brow crinkled. "Do models even smile anymore?"

Smile or not, he knew she would look stunning. "I'm not sure, but you're about to find out. Now, have you heard about the Jade Market they have here?"

SHELBY HAD a strong sense of déjà vu as she waited the next morning in the same chair as the previous night. Except this time, Misty was seated beside her, luggage already stowed in the town car.

"I'm sure I told William to be ready to leave by now." Impatiently, Misty glanced at her watch again. "And he got to bed at a reasonable hour?"

Why was she looking at her like she was the reason he might not have gotten much sleep? "Yeah, we went to the Jade Market after we ate and then came back to the hotel. I assume he went to bed like I did." A trickle of concern crept into her belly. *Maybe something had happened to him.*

"Ah, there you are, William. What kept you?" Misty waved at a stooped figure clutching his stomach as he made his way over to them. "Are you all right?"

Shelby peered closer at him, alarmed at Misty's words. The Billy who had finally emerged bore a scant resemblance to the hearty man of the night before. Now he was pale, sweating and trembling. "What happened?"

He raised bloodshot eyes to glare at her. "You're what happened."

Mystified at the accusation, she could only stare back at him. "I don't remember doing that to you."

"Remember when I wanted to go to the restaurant like a normal person, but you were all like, 'Billy, live a little'? Ring any bells?' His voice rose alarmingly.

"Yeah?" she said in a little voice.

"Well, I lived last night, curled up in the bathroom, too scared to so much as think of passing wind without being on the toilet for fear of soiling myself. Oh, that's before I even got started on the vomiting. You gave me food poisoning." He jabbed the air in front of her. Several guests were beginning to stop and stare at them.

"William, lower your voice, you're creating a scene," Misty hissed.

"I didn't create the scene. I'm the poor schmuck who's being forced to live it," he hissed back at her. "She's the one who created it."

Shelby thought his accusations were more than a little unfair. "But I ate exactly what you ate," she protested. "And you even agreed it was delicious." She felt horrible that he was ill, but there was no need to cast the blame at her doorstep.

"Well, obviously you're used to peasant food and I'm not." His eyes widened, a panicked look of terror flashing across his face. A moist gurgle pre-empted a groan of pure despair as fresh perspiration sprung out on his ashen forehead. With one hand pressed to his mouth and the other to his side, he frantically shuffled away, leaving a pungent aroma in his wake.

"What the heck did you get him to eat last night?" Misty waved her hand in an attempt to dispel the smell.

"Nothing that bad, honestly. He's a few pickles short of a barrel if he thinks he can blame that on me." But it didn't matter if she was to blame or not, he did. It was going to be one long, awkward smelly flight home.

CHAPTER 6

*T*he suit was quite simply a marvel of artistic sensibility, the way the shades of gray twirled together to form a pattern like oil on water. Mr Onissios had added a rather snazzy pink shirt to complete the outfit.

"So, my muse has agreed?" The way the designer said it, William thought that if he had been stroking a hairless cat, he would have made a perfect villain in a movie.

"Yes, after realizing what she could contribute, she found herself unable to refuse," Misty said, staring at the designer on the big screen in the conference room. Dana wordlessly placed a cup of coffee in front of her boss before quietly exiting the room. William wondered where his was. "I will forward a contract for Shelby and her rate as the face of the collection—and your belief that she is essential for the process therefore makes that rate non-negotiable." He'd seen the figure, and with Misty having decided to represent Shelby, the cowgirl was going to be very well compensated for her efforts.

"My muse is priceless." The designer twirled his hands in the air dismissively. "As a muse should be. Now, I will need her here in six weeks' time for the photoshoot. A week later, she will walk the show for me," Mr Onissios said.

"Six weeks? Are the dates negotiable?" Misty looked panicked.

"He can't change the date of the fashion show, that's the Paris Fashion Week," William answered for the other man.

"Okay, well then, unless there's anything we haven't covered, I think we can finish this up?" Misty looked between William and Mr Onissios for affirmation. "Thank you for your time, Mr Onissios. I look forward to seeing your designs for myself." The screen went blank. "Oh no, I can't be there for the photoshoot. The date clashes with an event I'm holding with Chora. I can make a day before the fashion show if I leave as soon as it finishes and let Chora take care of the final details."

William watched her take a sip of coffee to calm her jangled nerves. He decided he really should call his PA for one. Actually, where was she? This was the third one he'd had this month. Maybe he should try to steal Dana away from Misty. His lips twitched. *Like that would happen.*

"I'm sure Shelby will be fine. She's a big girl."

Misty turned baleful eyes to him. "You're only saying that after what happened in Myanmar."

Something horribly similar to guilt landed in his belly. "Maybe I overreacted a little bit," he grudgingly admitted. "I'm almost sure she didn't mean for that to happen. Anyway, I've forgiven her, and now it's best we never speak about that night and the return flight again—for everyone's sake." He still had nightmares about the return home. The more he thought about it, the more he began to worry that maybe Shelby wouldn't be okay going by herself. She was so open, and there was a good chance the fashion folk would eat her alive. The thought didn't sit comfortably with him. "Maybe I should accompany her?"

Misty looked at him like he'd suddenly grown another head. He was rather surprised at his offer himself. "Really? Just like that?"

"Well, I just bought an island and hired a new caretaker. I thought I could take your plane on a detour home and see if they're doing a good job. Anyway, you know I love fashion."

"I don't remember offering my plane."

"But you weren't planning on letting Shelby fly over commercial, were you? I thought you liked her." He affected a tone of horror, hand flying to his chest.

"Fine." She laughed. "You got me. You can take the plane. But I might need it to fly back and get me so I can see Shelby walk in the show. I'm sure Logan wouldn't want to miss it."

"And I wouldn't want to miss seeing what Paris thinks of your cowboy."

Maybe this trip to Paris was going to be more fun than he thought.

THE KITCHEN WAS SMALL, verging on almost too cozy, and yet nowhere else felt like home as much as this room did to Shelby. She sniffed appreciatively as her mother set a plate of raisin cookies down in front of her.

"Now, do you want to tell me why you're moping around my kitchen?" Her mom's gaze challenged her to deny it.

"I think I've changed my mind about modeling for Misty." There she'd said it. Shelby picked up a cookie and slowly began to crumb it between her fingers. Without so much as a shift in her expression, her mom removed it and placed it back on the plate.

"I thought you said the people were lovely and you wanted to help them."

Shelby focused on brushing the crumbs from her hands,

not wanting to meet her mother's gaze. Her voice was level, but she was sure she was going to see disappointment reflected back up at her if she were to chance a peek. "Yeah, and I do, but just, well, now they want me to walk in their clothes in front of people."

"Shelby Erikson, you've been walking since you were one year old, and a lot of that time it's been in front of people. Now tell me the real reason."

"Um, Misty can't come and now Billy is and, well, it didn't end so great the last time we met." Her cheeks burned in remembrance. She wasn't sure Billy was any keener to see her again than she was him. No, that wasn't true. She wished she could see him again. Just before the food poisoning explosion. The Billy whose eyes had twinkled at her with respectful surprise when she'd known about the beautiful exotic city they had been in.

"So, the man got ill and hurled his cookies up. You don't think your father hasn't done that? Is that the only reason you don't want to do it—because you're embarrassed?"

"It's a pretty big reason. It's not like we're on borrowing terms anymore." Scalded, Shelby looked up finding only love staring back at her in her mother's eyes. "I don't think I can do it."

Her mom took a cookie and bit down into it. Shelby watched as the crumbs fell neatly onto the plate. Silence stretched as she enjoyed the morsel, Shelby beginning to think her mom had let her off the hook and felt strangely empty that she'd gotten her own way when she laid it on her.

"What about all those kids and ladies you met?"

"Maybe they can get someone else to do it?" *Maybe a big-name supermodel.* The thought made her guilt lighten.

"I thought that fancy French designer said he'd only do it if he had you?"

"Yeah, but it's not like I'm some great name. Maybe if they

give him a better option than me, he'll see that's the better way to go."

"And if he doesn't? You're willing to let all those folk down because you're embarrassed to see a man again?" It sounded silly when her mom said it like that. Shelby squirmed under her mother's steady gaze. "When all they want you to do is have some pictures taken and walk a bit in some fancy clothes."

The guilt hardened again in her stomach. "I mean, when you say it like that."

"I think, Shelby, if you listen to your heart, you'll know what to do."

Shelby stared at her mother. Why did she feel worse than if she'd just received a dressing down? Sighing, she picked up another cookie. Looks like she was going to Paris. *This trip was going to be as much fun as hugging a bramble bush.*

CHAPTER 7

*S*eeing Billy sitting there reading a magazine, effortlessly chic and perfectly in control, made Shelby grind to a halt. Naively, she'd assumed she was boarding the flight first. Next time she was going to make sure to ask to be on the safe side. Awkwardly, she stood frozen in place, feeling as welcome as a skunk at a lawn party. How was it that this man made her catch her breath and want to crawl into a hole and hide all at the same time?

Sighing, Billy closed the magazine and looked up at her, the line of his mouth tightening a fraction. "Would you please sit down, Shelby? If you insist on standing for the entire flight to Paris, I'm going to get a sore neck from looking up at you."

Shelby scuttled to her seat opposite his, knowing the smile she gave the hostess as she took her carry-on luggage was a little too tight, her eyes too stressed. Her mom had always said that she could talk under water with a mouthful of marbles, but now the well had truly and completely run dry. Maybe she could close her eyes and pretend to go to sleep, the good Lord knew she was tired enough.

"Shelby, I owe you an apology." She gaped, raising her eyes to find him staring at her. Billy rubbed the back of his neck. "And don't look at me like that. It makes me feel worse than I already do. Look, I was out of line with what I said. I let my temper get the better of me and I shouldn't have. Maybe I'm more like my father than I'd like." Shelby wondered at his last words. It was the first time she'd ever heard him mention his family. There was an air of isolation to him that she'd never noticed before. "Anyway, I shouldn't have said what I did. I didn't mean it, and I don't think it was your fault at all. I actually had a good time until, well, I didn't." Billy shuddered, no doubt lost in excruciating remembrance.

The pristine white leather of her armrest was warm from the sun filtering in through the window as she drew circles against it. "I felt really bad about what happened."

"Then how about we promise never to talk about it again?"

They exchanged a subtle look of amusement, giddy relief making her feel lightheaded. "I'd like that. And while we're making promise, I have one more I'd like to give. When we're in Paris, I promise to let you make all the decisions about what we eat."

"My belly and I thank you."

There was a trace of laughter to his voice. Shelby picked up the romance novel she'd brought with her, causing his brows to rise in surprise, but otherwise he didn't say anything. Opening it to her bookmark, she was filled with a warm glow. Maybe her mother was right. If she listened to her heart, she'd be just fine.

As she stared around the sumptuous room she'd just entered, it seemed like she was going to be more than fine. Shelby gaped at the understated black and white opulence surrounding her. Everywhere she looked, little touches spoke of elegance and class … and a lot of money. The clean lines with the added refinement of lacquer of the dressing screens or the velvet of the cushions and drapes, the discreet touches of gold or the marble fireplace.

"I didn't even know people lived like this," she breathed, thankful Billy was inspecting his room and wasn't there to see her catching flies like a country bumpkin.

Shelby's phone began to ring, reminding her she'd promised to call her mother once they'd safely landed. "Hey, Mom, sorry I forgot to call."

"I'll pass that on." Shelby twitched at Misty's voice. "Or maybe as soon as we finish talking, you should call her."

"That might be a good idea."

"So, what do you think of Paris?"

How to answer that? The city she'd seen through the car window as they'd been driven to the Hotel Ritz had oozed sophistication. Self-consciously, she fiddled with the end of her braid, painfully aware that she was makeup-free and her hair was in dire need of some attention, and yet the city sang its siren song to her, whispering of delights if only she would step outside.

"It's not like back home," she said lamely.

"I should hope not." Misty laughed. "You've been on a plane an awful long time just to end up back in Texas. Are you in your suite?"

"Yes, I got in a few minutes ago."

"Do you like it?"

"It makes me feel like I should be in satin pajamas, swanning around with a glass of champagne and a poodle trotting by my side."

More laughter down the phone. "If you do, I want to see photos. You're in the Coco Chanel suite. William insisted it be booked for you." Shelby listened with bewilderment, the thought making her belly give an odd little flip flop. Why would it matter to him what room she had? "Now, on to the real reason I'm calling."

"I thought it was because you love your one-day sister-in-law?"

"That too. Logan and I will be there in two days' time. Basically, my pilot is coming straight back to collect us. We'll be flying out after Chora's event."

"Will you be here for the photoshoot?" Nerves jangled painfully at the thought of what was to come, but if Misty and Logan were there, then maybe it wouldn't be too bad. She thought about her brother watching, no doubt making fun of her. Maybe Misty could leave him at the hotel.

"No, we'll miss that." *Maybe it was for the best.* "But we'll definitely be there for the big fashion show. I'm so excited. Do you know that I've never had front row tickets for a show at the Paris Fashion Week?" Misty's words vibrated with excitement. Personally, Shelby felt sick thinking about it. "Anyway, Dana's telling me I have to get off the phone because you and William have an appointment to meet with Mr Onissios. Yes, Dana, I'm saying goodbye now." Shelby could imagine the PA waving her hands in the background. "Okay, have fun, and I'll see you in a few days." And the line went dead.

Shelby stood in the middle of the room, eyeing the purity of the contents. She felt like a bull in a china shop, or at least a cowgirl standing in the middle of the Coco Chanel suite. Her gaze darted to her nails, just to be sure she'd removed all the grease from beneath them. Reaching down, she took off her cowboy boots and, holding them in front of her, made her way to the bathroom on sock clad feet. She didn't want to take any chances that she might be trekking dirt from the barn back home across Coco's carpets.

IT WAS a surprise to find the usually nattily dressed designer with pins between his teeth and shirt sleeves rolled up when William and Shelby entered his design studio. For some reason, William had had it in his mind that the man created his visions on paper and then had his minions do the work. His respect for Mr Onissios—already high—rose significantly.

Waving the androgynous assistant away, the great man himself walked over to greet them. Well, Shelby, more like it. William could only watch in amused amazement as he gathered her by the elbows and kissed each cheek, Shelby looking like she'd stepped into another dimension. He moved slightly to block off any escape if she were to bolt from the room. Either that or he'd follow right after her.

"My muse, you're finally here," crowed Mr Onissios. "Now my visions, they come to life."

"Um, cool." Shelby hunched her shoulders, drawing in on herself uncertainly.

"Mr Onissios is a creative," William explained, stepping closer to Shelby, almost touching, but not quite. He could feel her lean in closer, the space between them diminishing as if drawing comfort from him. "He can be a little flamboyant."

"Oh purlease." The designer fluttered his hands in the air. "That is like saying Mount Everest is a small hill. I own my drama and I'm worth every penny it brings."

A tight giggle escaped Shelby. She was still nervous, but it was a relief that she seemed to be functioning again. "My mom has a saying you might like."

"My darling muse, educate me," Mr Onissios commanded, resting his chin on the back of his hands, gazing adoringly at her.

Shelby flickered a dazed look at William. He gave her a reassuring wink. *You've got this, Shelby, just be you.* "Um," she cleared her throat. "She says in situations like this that she'd like to buy him for what he's worth and sell him for what he thinks he'll bring."

"I must meet this woman." Mr Onissios waved a finger in the air. "She will sit beside me and whisper such words to me."

Shelby laughed, the tension easing from her body. "I'm not sure she's the whispering kind. She's noisier than a restless mule in a tin shed. Plus, Dad wouldn't let her whisper to any man other than him."

The designer sighed forlornly. "My heart will never recover. Now, my assistant, Xandi, will help you get into the first outfit. We will check for fit and repeat."

The impossibly thin Xandi materialized again and escorted Shelby to behind a curtained area. William was proud of her. She'd been herself and won over Mr Onissios. He knew it would be the first of many. That was the thing about Shelby—she didn't seem like she was doing much, and the next thing you knew, you'd let your guard down. She might actually be more dangerous than Misty. A low laugh sounded from the dressing area, rusty from lack of use. William had been treated to Shelby laughing before—it was infectious and freely given—and he was fairly certain it wasn't her. But if it wasn't her, then that meant...

Surely it wasn't the dour-faced Xandi. She didn't look like she found anything amusing.

The two women stepped out from behind the curtain, the woman accompanying Shelby giving her a tentative smile as though she was using a muscle she'd forgotten she had. William smiled to himself. Shelby really was something else. Eyes opening wide, he took in the vision before him. The gown Shelby wore was black with intricate embroidery over it in reds and yellows. The bodice was slashed to the sternum with a daring front slit, and cap sleeves hung gracefully from her shoulder. It had been made just for her by a master designer from the most expensive fabric in the world and it showed.

She was stunning, not a trace of the cowgirl remaining. Shyly, she raised her eyes to his, a question shimmering as if no matter what the mirror told her, she needed to see it reflected back at her from his gaze. A sense of responsibility for the power she had given him made him pause. Holding his hand over his heart, William bowed. The joy radiating from her at the gesture far exceeded the simple move.

Mr Onissios clapped his hands together. "My muse, I pictured how this would look on you every day I designed it. And now to see in the flesh, my heart is happy that you and only you will wear it."

"Thank you, Mr Onissios. This dress is—" Shelby gave a helpless shrug. "I don't know that I will ever wear something so perfect in my life again. Thank you." She looked like a goddess, and yet she was the one who felt honored. William knew the world didn't deserve Shelby Erikson.

The thought remained with him all through the rest of the fitting and discussions of the upcoming photoshoot. When they finally emerged, the sky had darkened into night. Shelby's stomach gave a rumble. "I should've known you would be hungry." William gently steered her to the other side of the street by her elbow, keeping his hand in place once they were safely across.

"It's a lot harder to stand around getting pins stuck into you and being told how beautiful you are than I thought." Mischief twinkled from her eyes. "It's exhausting." Another rumble interrupted her, and she giggled. "And gives you quite an appetite."

"Lucky for you, I know a lovely little café. I discovered it years ago when I first came here. It's a bit of a local secret, but I think I can trust you not to tell."

"Who would I tell? It's not like I'll be back anytime soon."

William was caught off-guard by her words. "Why wouldn't you be back in Paris? Don't you like it?"

She turned shining eyes to him as they continued to walk. "I love it. It has this vibe that's amazing and just makes you want to completely immerse yourself in it." Shelby wrinkled her nose. "You must think I'm an idiot, and I know I'm not describing it very well, but it's intoxicating." William couldn't agree more. Watching the passion emanate from her was quite simply the most intoxicating thing he'd ever seen.

"Then if you love it so much, why won't you be back?" He gestured around at the tree-lined street, the uniquely Parisian shopfronts, their windows reflecting their images back at them as they passed, and the fashionably dressed men and women who ambled by. It saddened him that Shelby didn't think she would return to this magical city.

It was like watching the sun go behind the clouds, her expression wistful. "Because this is a bit of a fairytale, isn't it? Tomboy cowgirl gets plucked from obscurity and whisked away to Paris to be told she's beautiful. But we all know that when midnight strikes, I'll go back to being plain old Shelby, and poof, all of this will go away."

William stopped walking and pulled her to the side of the walkway, out of the way of the people headed to destinations unknown. He turned to face her. "Shelby, I think you'll find that you won't ever go back to being plain old Shelby. You never were. And this taste of life you're experiencing, it's only the tip of the iceberg—if you want it."

There was a spark of some indefinable emotion in her eyes. "I don't know if I want that either. I liked my life back home, too. You know, I'm terrified that I'm going to let all those lotus silk women down. That any time now everyone's going to realize I'm an imposter."

He cupped her chin, putting all the faith he had in her in his gaze. The intensity with which he wanted her to know just how special she was surprised him. "You won't let them down, I promise."

Shelby gave a nod as though not quite believing him, but not willing to disagree. They resumed walking down the street. "I don't really get any of this—what makes one thing fashionable and another not. I thought clothes just needed to be functional."

"First, there's a big difference between trendy and fashion. A trend is fleeting, but fashion, it's a completely different beast. You take Mr Onissios for example, he can look at a piece of fabric and know how it's going to drape when he cuts it and the colors that will take pretty to exquisite. He understands the female form and how to dress it. That is a gift, and it is people like him who create true fashion."

"I didn't know that," Shelby quietly admitted. "Did your mom teach you about fashion?"

Pensively, he stared down the street. How to describe a woman he only remembered in the shadows of half-forgotten memories? "I didn't know my mother." He felt, rather than heard, Shelby's soft intake of breath. "She left me and didn't want anything more to do with me." Knife-sharp pain had long become a dull numbness.

"I'm so sorry, William. I didn't know."

His lips quirked at her finally calling him by his real name. "It's not something I advertise." Strange that now she'd said it, it no longer seemed to sound right, not on her lips at least. "You don't have to call me William. I've gotten used to Billy."

A smile found its way through her mask of uncertainty. "You always seemed more like a Billy to me."

"Then Billy it is." He opened the door to the café they'd stopped in front of. "And I believe you'll make a difference for those women. I don't believe in much—mainly in money —but I believe in you." He recognized the simple truth in his words. William couldn't remember the last time he'd believed in someone who wasn't him. *It was nice.*

CHAPTER 8

*L*ight spilled through in golden shafts as the maid opened the curtains. Delicate cup of hot chocolate in hand, William made his way out onto the terrace and took in the view overlooking the Place Vendôme. It had become his tradition to partake of the velvety, thick beverage whenever in Paris. It was a million miles away from the hot cocoa on offer back in New York. Breathing in deeply, he settled himself on the outdoor lounge, puzzling over the unfamiliar feeling lingering over him. Taking a sip of his drink, William let out a long sigh of contentment. If he wasn't careful, he might get used to this bottomless sense of peace and satisfaction. It was almost like he was happy.

Chuckling at the stupendousness of this new development, he opened his phone and began to peruse his emails. One from Misty was flagged urgent. A frisson of unease shot up his spine at the thought of something having gone wrong and impacting on Shelby's collection. Grimly, he opened it.

I told you to leave Shelby alone. I'm not sure what Logan's going to say.

Below it was a link. Baffled, he clicked on it and a news

article popped open. William took a deep breath of utter astonishment. Underneath a headline of *The Billionaire Bachelor and The Next Big Thing* was a picture of him and Shelby from the night before. At least he assumed it was. Peering closer, he could make out the shops behind them. It was definitely the night before when he'd pulled her aside. It was strange looking at that moment from the outside. He stood with his hand gently caressing Shelby's cheek, their eyes locked together as if no one else was around, two souls in perfect harmony in that single instant.

Startled, he realized they looked like star-crossed lovers. He wrinkled his nose. He'd been in Paris too long if he was beginning to have flights of fancy like that. William paused, considering if Shelby was awake and if she'd seen it yet. Deciding the answers were yes and no, he gathered his cup and, with a last deep breath on his terrace, went in search of her.

Standing at the threshold of the door to her suite, his smile broadened into approval as he took in Shelby's appearance. Long pajama bottoms, an old T-shirt and messy hair—and she wore all of it well. William wasn't sure when he'd seen a sexier outfit in his life. Shelby, on the other hand, didn't seem as thrilled to see him as he did her. Her eyes widened in alarm and for a brief moment it seemed like she was going to slam the door shut in his face. Deciding to head that line of action off, he pushed the door open with the palm of his hand and sauntered in.

"Good morning, Shelby. How did you sleep last night?" Urbanely, he took a sip of his by now cold hot chocolate.

"Um, like a log." She tugged at her shirt before crossing her arms over her chest. "I wasn't expecting you before breakfast."

He gave her an extravagant wink. "It was such a beautiful

morning and I thought to myself, why should Shelby miss out on it?"

"Oh." She seemed to still be groggy. "Sorry, I haven't had my coffee yet."

"Let's fix that. And then I have something to show you."

William was surprised at the way her eyes narrowed as she glared at him. "The last man who said that to me ended up hogtied in a chicken coop. I thought better of you."

He blinked. *What on earth?* "You've lost me. But whatever it is you think I'm about to show you, it's not."

"Is this where you tell me that what you have is special, like nothing I've ever seen before? That dog won't hunt here." Shelby began to make a shooing gesture with her hands. "I think you can leave now."

William finally cottoned on to what Shelby thought he was implying. He didn't know whether to laugh or be offended by her reaction. "Shelby, you've got it all wrong. I assume you haven't received an email from Misty?"

She ceased her shooing and stared at him, mouth pressed in an uncompromising line. "No."

He held out his phone. "You might want to read this article."

It was intriguing watching the gambit of emotions chase themselves across her tanned face. Suspicion, curiosity, shock, and then abject dismay. "But we aren't—you and me. They've got it all wrong," she said, flabbergasted. "You were just being nice to me."

There was a tone of resignation that made him look closer at her and he wondered what he might be missing. "That's the media for you. Always looking for a story, and if they don't know the truth, they'll make it up."

Shelby's hand flew to her mouth. "Did you say Misty sent this to you? Does that mean Logan's seen this? What about my dad and mom? I don't want them getting the wrong idea."

Okay, that hurt a little. Why would it matter if her parents saw this and thought it was true? He was quite the catch, and multiple magazines articles could confirm it. "I don't know who else has seen it. Probably Dana, but you don't really know her, so that doesn't matter." William tried to keep his tone neutral. "This is out there. You've seen it, and now we can move on. It might even be a good thing."

"How is this a good thing?" Her voice was breathless, a question he couldn't quite figure out hidden in her words.

"Well, it's publicity for the collection, and that interest is going to help sell it. On that note, have some breakfast and get ready."

"For what? I thought I didn't have anything scheduled today?"

"You don't. But you can't come to Paris and not do some shopping."

"But what happens if there's more paparazzi out there?"

"Then we'll ignore them like any celebrity worth their salt would do and continue on with our day."

She seemed reassured by his suggestion and nodded. "Give me half an hour."

IT BEGAN to dawn on Shelby as she strolled past the cafés that maybe one could—and perhaps should—have more in their wardrobe than jeans and tees. The last dress she'd purchased had been for Colt and Evelyn's wedding, and that had been selected online at the eleventh hour by her mom and she'd even recycled it for her trip to Myanmar. Watching the Parisiennes go about their lives, there was an elegance that was hard to define but nonetheless present in all of them. It wasn't that they dressed like girly girls either, but they were about as similar to her as an elephant to a swan.

Putting her hands dejectedly into her jean pockets, she looked up to find Billy staring at her. Great, what had she done to embarrass herself now? "What?"

"I was just thinking." Billy regarded her with a speculative gleam.

"About what?' Gosh, she sounded like a petulant brat.

"About you, Shelby Erikson." The way he said her name sent a warm shiver spiraling into her belly. "I think it's time we mean business and get to shopping."

"Oh, I can't really afford anything, so I'm happy to just tag along."

"Haven't you realized the perks of having a billionaire as a friend yet?" A happy little glow filled her as she processed his words. *He considered them friends*. After the rocky start they'd had, it was more than she'd hoped for and yet, greedily, she wished he felt more. "And I think you'll find that I'm very generous to my friends." Billy linked his arm with hers. "Now let's get shopping."

It didn't take very long for Shelby to realize that Billy took shopping very seriously. They would enter a store, and from the way the sullen looking attendants' eyes would widen first with surprise and then a cunning gleam, it was clear they knew who he was. Next, he would assume an exaggerated bored expression—at least, she thought he assumed it, it was kind of hard to tell. A series of commands were issued next, and it changed depending on what store they were in, but it was always around a silhouette, fabric or color, and heaven help if they went rogue and didn't follow it to a tee. A cutting glance of rebuke was swiftly dispensed at the disappointing party and he no longer paid them the least bit of attention. When the garments or accessories had been assembled as per his request, he'd sit down and indicate for Shelby to go into the dressing room and try them on.

She very nearly had a heart attack as she turned over the

price tag on a simple jersey wrap dress. Holy heck, it was more than her weekly wage and then some. As she slipped it on and tied it snuggly around her waist, she gazed wide-eyed at her reflection. It had never bothered Shelby all that much that she didn't have lots of curves. She'd long gotten used to being tall and athletically lean. But somehow the miracle of a dress gave her the shape of a woman. The cinched waist emphasized the swelling of her hips and modest bust. The delicate lavender and gold pattern made her tan glow richly against it. Her hand crept to touch her hair as she stared unbelievingly at her reflection like she needed to make sure it really was her.

"Excuse me, mademoiselle, is everything to your liking?" the lyrical voice of the attendant asked through the curtain.

"Um, yes, thank you. I'm about to come out." *Would Billy think she looked different from before?* Taking a deep breath, she swept the fabric aside and walked out.

His appreciative gaze traveled from her bare feet to the top of her head. The look so intimate it left a trailing warmth as if he touched her. Shelby could feel her color rising under his perusal, and his gaze came to rest on her questioning eyes. "I think Paris will be the making of you. If you're not careful, you might never want to get back into jeans and cowboy boots again."

"Oh, I could never turn my back on them, but this"—she smoothed the fabric down over her hips—"well, if I'm not careful, I'm liable to break my arm patting myself on the back, it's that pretty."

"Excellent." Billy turned to the attendant. "We'll take it, je vous remercie." He returned his attention to Shelby. "And you were just happy to tag along. The next shop, we are going to do the most divine coats." His eyes narrowed as he looked intently at her. "I'm thinking red."

"Red is a bold color." At least that's what her mom always said.

Billy winked at her. "Then it's a good thing you're a bold woman."

Shelby literally could not think of a single reply to his statement. Flustered, she slung back into the cubicle to change.

TIME and again William found his gaze traveling back to Shelby of its own free will. Seeing her in the high-end fashion, now she would stand out in any room she walked into. But maybe she always would have. One just needed to really see what they were looking at, know its value. The sharp intake of breath beside him was the only warning he had before she darted from his side and across the road. How she wasn't hit by a scooter and several cars was beyond him. Prudently, he waited for it to be safe before he crossed to join her.

"Have you seen anything as beautiful in your life?"

"No, I don't think I ever have," William truthfully answered, staring at the glorious woman standing in front of him—or kneeling, as the case may be—as she reverently ran her hand inches away from the panel of a car, apparently too scared to touch it.

"I've read about these. It was the first to break Bugatti's record of three hundred and four miles per hour." His heart leapt into his throat as she turned glowing eyes to him, a beatific smile beaming at full force. She thrust her phone at him. "Quick, take a picture of me standing beside it."

William wondered what the owner would make of him taking a photo of their car. He smiled ruefully. He probably knew them. Shelby got herself into position and smiled, keeping a careful distance from herself and the object of her worshipful gaze. "It's pretty quick, then?"

Shelby gave him a reproachful glance for daring to make light of the car. "The SSC Tuatara only goes three hundred and sixteen miles per hour. So, I'd say pretty fast. Anyway, a gal can dream. I think the base models go for 1.9 million dollars and then it's up from there."

"You know, if modeling works out for you, you could buy one for yourself." William found himself casting an eye around, looking for any other cars that might generate the level of excitement in Shelby as this one. He wondered if he'd ever been as innocent as she was, finding joy in everything around her.

"I think I need to survive my first photoshoot before we start spending money I don't have."

"But a top model earns enough to live a life of luxury, affording what they want," he pressed.

"I'm pretty happy with the life I have."

"But if money wasn't a problem, isn't there anything you really want?" It was strangely important for him to know.

Shelby looked almost guilty as she looked around before leaning in closer. "A Shelby Cobra. Because I mean, it's like it was made for me."

William couldn't quite stop the smile spreading across his face. "It sounds like it."

"I know, right?" She nodded energetically. "Do you mind if we don't do any more shopping today? I don't think I can handle another wardrobe change."

"Do you think you could handle a drink back at the hotel?"

"Only if I'm sitting down." Her eyes twinkled mischievously back at him.

"I think that can be arranged."

Shelby linked her arm with his. "Then why are we standing here?"

William was still studying the way Shelby made him feel as he waited for their drinks to arrive. She wasn't classically beautiful or the stereotypical blonde bombshell. Her smile was a little too wide, cute freckles sprinkled over her face, and her look a little too direct. But there was no denying that she was magnetically glorious in her imperfections. He smiled as their drinks were placed in front of them.

"Billy, I don't think I've ever had a martini," Shelby confessed.

"There's no time like the present." He removed the olive from the toothpick it was skewered on with his teeth, enjoying the saltiness against his tongue. Curiously, he watched Shelby take her first tentative sip.

She gave a spluttering cough that she tried to stifle. Clearing her throat, she gave a little nod. "It's strong, but nice." As if to prove her point, she took another drink, this time swallowing with only a slight choking noise.

"I can get you something else if you'd like?"

Shelby waved his suggestion aside. "My mama didn't raise no quitter."

"I don't imagine she did." William wrapped his fingers around the cold lump in his pocket. He was going to miss having it with him. "I have something for you." Slowly, he withdrew it and placed it on the table.

Shelby's pale blue eyes shimmered as she stared at the intricately carved jade horse. "It's beautiful." A memory flickered to life in her gaze. "Is that the one we saw in Myanmar? At the Jade Markets?' Astonished disbelief furrowed her brows. "You got it for me?"

The way she was staring at him, it was like he'd gotten her a priceless diamond. The idea of how she'd react if he actually did get her diamonds was tantalizing. "I'm not sure what made me get it." Where had his suaveness gone? His words were as clumsy as a schoolboy talking to his first crush. "But I thought you might like it."

"Like it?" Shelby cradled the little horse protectively in her hands. "I love it." She smiled as she spoke, her eyes luminous. "Thank you."

William couldn't remember the last time he'd felt so good. It was addictive.

CHAPTER 9

There had to be a word for the trembling feeling of uncertainty that made Shelby not know whether she wanted to flee to the toilet or vomit. Maybe the French had one for it. If they did, it probably sounded terribly chic and sophisticated. Either way, Shelby wasn't filled with bright and fuzzies as she stepped into the studio for her photoshoot. The first thing that struck her was how many more people than she'd been expecting were in the room. She counted four standing around the camera equipment, another fussing with clothing, and three over by what looked to be the makeup and hair section, judging by the mirrors and highchairs. A tall, thin platinum-blonde glared at her from one of the said chairs. Such was the intensity in the glare that Shelby racked her brain trying to remember if she'd ever met the woman before, let alone offended her. Shuffling her feet, she came up blank.

A gentle but firm hand on the small of her back nudged her forward, and a warm breath tickled her ear. "You know, you have to eventually enter the room to have a photoshoot." Shelby could hear the laughter in Billy's voice.

69

"Can't they just shoot me from here?" Why had she ever thought this was going to be a good idea? She was a Texan cowgirl and a mechanic to boot, not some fancy model. She didn't belong in this world. Visions of children sadly sitting outside the closed lotus silk workshops, their eyes reproachful, taunted her. "Mama didn't raise no quitter," she muttered under her breath, lifting her chin and striding forward.

"Good girl," Billy said approvingly, matching her steps, neither in front nor behind her, but perfectly parallel. It was like he was there solely in a supporting role, not seeking to take control. It dawned on her that Billy viewed it as her moment, but dear Lord she wished she could trail in his wake and let him bear the brunt of the attention.

"Shelby, my muse. My heart sings with delight at what we will capture today with the camera." Mr Onissios greeted her, grasping her arms and pulling her forward for him to kiss each cheek. "I trust William has been taking care of you."

"According to the papers, she's had his undivided attention," the model said with a heavy Russian accent. Maybe that's why Shelby felt like she was making fun of her.

"I saw the pictures. Shelby, you looked glorious. It only further impressed upon me that you were the right choice to be my muse." Mr Onissios clearly had zero qualms about Billy's attention and where he chose to lay them.

"And yet, wasn't I once your favorite model?" The blonde's eyes narrowed, making her beautiful features hard. Shelby thought she wouldn't age particularly well.

"Yes, a favorite model, never a muse. That is something a designer, if he is lucky, gets once—maybe twice—in a lifetime." Mr Onissios linked his arm with Shelby and gave a shooing gesture at the Russian woman. "They can finish your look once Shelby has been done. She's the priority today." With a haughty toss of her blonde head, she rose from her chair and, with an exaggerated leg-crossing action, strode off. The designer pursed his lips disapprovingly. "You'll have to ignore Annika. She's used to being the top dog—one who doesn't particularly enjoy sharing the spotlight or her paramours."

"I didn't know there would be other models here." Shelby wasn't quite sure what paramour meant, but she was going to look it up the first chance she got.

"I am sorry that no one thought to tell you, but we decided that, to give the collection the best chance of succeeding, it was best to pair you—a new face—with an established name." He gestured at the blonde who'd made her way to Billy. "Annika."

Shelby wasn't sure she liked the way Annika had sidled up to Billy, eyeing him like a hungry hog at the trough as Mr Onissios left her in the hands of the stylists to be primped and preened.

"That one never did understand when a man wasn't interested. If a man has a taste of the cake and doesn't come back for more, then that has to tell you that something must be very off in the batter," the makeup artist said as she began to gather her tools. The woman had bright, fluro-green hair fashioned into a mohawk. Shelby knew she was being rude, but she couldn't help staring at the architectural marvel. The woman flashed her an impish grin. "I know, it's awesome, right?"

Shelby found herself giving her an answering grin. "It sure is something. I'm Shelby, by the way." She held her hand out.

The makeup artist juggled her palette and brush, taking Shelby's hand in a firm grasp. "I'm Suzie, and I know you're kinda the main attraction around here." She held a finger to her lips. "Just don't tell Annika." She cocked her brightly colored head to one side, her lips pursed as she stared at the tall blonde. "Or maybe we should. I'd enjoy watching her head explode when she heard the news." Shelby wasn't sure her mom would approve of the thoughts she was having about what she'd like to see happen to Annika, especially if she didn't stop running her fingers up Billy's arm. Suzie gave a snort of disgust beside her. "Like I said, she clearly doesn't know when she isn't wanted."

Her words sparked keen interest in Shelby, and she turned slowly so as not to get a brush to the eye. "What do you mean?"

Suzie's eyes sparkled with the intense joy of being the first one to pass on juicy gossip to the new girl. "Well, Annika and William had a thing." She pursed her lips and stared a little into the distance. "I mean, I'm not even sure if you could call it that. It was a blink and you'd miss it kinda deal. Obviously, our Annika over there didn't get the memo. Can you please close your eyes?"

Stunned, Shelby complied. She'd assumed Billy had had girlfriends, but to be confronted by it here without any warning seemed cruel. A sourness settled in the pit of her stomach. She opened betrayed eyes to stare at the two beautiful people standing together.

"Oh, sorry, did I get something in your eye?" Suzie asked solicitously.

It was only when Suzie dabbed at the tears trickling down her face that Shelby realized she'd been crying. "It's okay. I must just be a little sensitive." *That was the understatement of the year!*

"You should've said something," Suzie admonished. "I would've used something a little gentler from the beginning. But better late than never." Shelby let the makeup artist's words drift over her head, lost in a world of her own misery.

She was still numbly floating along, letting them dress her like a doll, when Mr Onissios came over to check she was turned out to his exacting expectations. Annika tore herself away from Billy and trailed after him. "A little here"—he tugged the neckline a fraction over—"a little bit more here"—a twitch to the hemline—"and voila, perfection."

"I'm not sure about that." Annika raised a condescending brow at Shelby. "I thought I would be wearing that piece."

"Annika, my dear. This is a key piece of the collection and I designed it for my muse. Are you saying my collection is not perfection?" Mr Onissios's voice was icy. Shelby shivered being so close to the frostiness. The designer waited, brow cocked, waiting impatiently for a response.

"No, of course your work is perfection, as usual," Annika hastily responded. Flustered, her gaze dropped to her feet.

Mr Onissios returned his attention to Shelby, taking a few steps back to take in his masterpiece. "It is my vision come to life."

Shelby grew warm under the compliment. "I feel like I'm in a dream."

"That's the only thing that explains you being here," Annika snidely muttered.

"More to the point, why are you still here?" Mr Onissios asked, not even bothering to look in the Russian's direction. "If you are not ready in five minutes, you're no longer part of this shoot." He stopped his admiration of Shelby to give Annika a sweetly fake smile. "And if that happens, I'll make sure to let everyone know how unprofessional you were." Annika glowered at Shelby before spinning on her heel and marching over toward Suzie. "Excuse me, I need to make sure that one doesn't cause any more mischief." Mr Onissios frowned peevishly as he followed in her wake.

Shelby let out a cramped breath, trying not to cry. Who was she kidding? She didn't belong here.

"I knew that dress would look amazing on you when you had the fitting, but now seeing you standing here with hair and makeup done, it blows my mind." There was a slight tinge of wonder to Billy's voice. His words that should have filled her with happiness now served to only leave her feeling miserable. "Is everything all right?"

Shelby continued to stare at her hands. She didn't dare trust herself to speak in case she embarrassed herself and started wailing like a baby. A gentle hand tenderly raised her chin. Slowly, she found herself staring into his magnetic gaze. "Shelby, what happened?"

"I just don't think, maybe, it's—" She knew her words were jumbled and not making sense, but still Billy didn't release her.

"Breathe for me, Shelby. Nice big breaths, in and out." He demonstrated as he spoke and Shelby found herself following his lead, calm flowing in with each inhale. Unfortunately, none of her misery left with the exhales. "Better?" She gave a little nod. He must think she was such an idiot. "Do you want to tell me what happened?"

"It's just now that I'm in the room with a real model, I think this has maybe all been a mistake. I'm not going to fool anyone. No one's going to believe I belong here." Humiliated, she dropped her gaze. Again, that gentle hand raised her back up.

"You're right." Billy's words stung. "You're not going to fool anyone. What everyone will see is what I see. A captivating, beautiful woman. Someone who isn't a model. Someone who's so much more. Don't sell yourself short by trying to pretend to be just like her"—he jabbed a thumb dismissively in Annika's direction—"or like me. You're real, you own everything about yourself, not like us." There was an air of isolation to him as he spoke, and for the first time she wondered if he was lonely.

"I'm not sure I believe what you said, but thanks. I needed to hear that." Shelby leaned forward and gave him a quick kiss on the cheek. Embarrassed by her impulsiveness, she pulled back, her cheeks heating.

That gentle hand stroked her cheek this time, the burn where he touched her skin intensifying. Bewildered, she peered at him through her lashes. His gaze back at her was as soft as a caress. Was he going to kiss her?

"Mr Onissios wants you to come over and talk to the photographer. Apparently, you have never worked a shoot before." Annika's tone might have been bored, but her eyes cut into Shelby like jagged glass. Mortified, she stepped away, stammering something unintelligible before escaping, her heart pounding in her chest. She was never going to be able to look Billy in the face again!

THE CAMERA LOVED HER! It was possible that William had never been prouder of someone in his entire life. The lighting captured the angles of her face and turned them into pure artistry. Shelby had started off hesitantly with Annika constantly jostling her for the prime position, but Mr Onissios wasn't going to have any of that. Between firm reprimands for the Russian model and constant praise and encouragement to Shelby, she'd emerged from her cocoon like the glorious butterfly he'd only half suspected had been hidden inside.

He found himself smiling at her over his drink at dinner that night. Shelby shot him a wary look, like a deer caught in the spotlight, unsure yet if it was by a friend or foe. Her fork halted mid-journey to her mouth. "What?"

"I was just thinking how well you did today at the photoshoot."

Surprised, he watched her expression become shuttered. "Oh, thanks."

He tried again. "You owned that shoot. I've seen seasoned supermodels do worse, and I'm not sure I've seen any do better."

Shelby appeared to be intently focused on the food on her plate as she chewed, and he only half caught what she muttered under her breath, but it sounded suspiciously like, "You would know." *What was that supposed to mean?*

Maybe he'd offended her when he'd nearly kissed her. It wasn't like he'd been planning to do it. It had just almost happened. William had noticed that about her. People just seemed to gravitate toward her, and he wasn't any exception. Maybe the pull he felt toward her was stronger than most, because he found himself seeing or reading something and wanting to tell her, to see her response. He loved how genuine she was. If it pleased her, her entire body would glow with delight, eyes shining at him as if they shared a secret. Confusion would send pink blossoming on her cheeks as she scrunched up her nose.

He still didn't know what, exactly, had happened at the photoshoot to make her look at him like he'd just told her a puppy had died, but he would get to the bottom of it. Maybe trying to kiss her hadn't been the smartest of moves, but he didn't regret it at all. No, that wasn't true. He regretted being interrupted and not actually kissing Shelby. Maybe next time he needed to try harder.

CHAPTER 10

*M*isty waltzed into William's suite like she owned the place. It shouldn't have surprised him that she'd managed to get a staff member to let her in—she spent almost as much time here as he did. He made a show of looking behind her. "Did you forget to pack your cowboy?"

"Very funny." She reached a hand languidly up to remove her sunglasses and that's when the light hit the giant diamond on her ring finger.

"Is that what I think it is?"

"If you think it's a very expensive piece of jewelry, you'd be right." Misty looked disgustingly satisfied. He was happy for her. She deserved it. "And Logan is checking in with Shelby. Did he mention anything about it to you?"

"About you getting here early? I didn't know rodeo clowns got paid so well." The line fell empty without Logan nearby to rile. William hoped Shelby didn't mention the almost kiss. If he was going to get hit by an overprotective brother, he at least wanted the kiss first!

"So you've pointed out before. Logan sold his car to buy

this, not that I'd have minded whatever he got me." She waved his comments aside. "I'm trying to find out who was in on it. Chora and Dana had everything under control for the first time ever for a gala and insisted that I be here to support Shelby. But I now suspect Logan had them in on his proposal scheme."

"I'm not entirely sure that you can refer to being proposed to as a scheme." William pulled Misty into an embrace. "Congratulations, my darling. I hope you made him sweat a little before putting him out of his misery."

Misty flashed him a guilty glance. "Maybe just a little bit."

"Is she telling you about my plane proposal?" Logan asked as he let himself in, Shelby trailing behind him. It struck William that Logan still looked every inch the cowboy, but his sister no longer fit the same mold. Sure, she still wore denim, but now wore a classic navy and white striped shirt with it and added a scarf jauntily tied around her neck. Now there was an air of refinement to her. Who knows? She might even start a new fashion trend of the Parisian Cowgirl.

Shelby peered at her brother in bafflement at his pronouncement. "What plane proposal?"

"You know how much Misty loves that plane of hers—I think it's her first love. Anyway, she's always in a good mood when she's on it, so I thought I would hedge the bets in my favor and ask while she was in the best possible mood. I got the crew to help out and filled the back of it with flowers and rose petals, then I went to use the bathroom, got into position, and then I released the stewardess."

Misty laughed. "He makes it sound like he's releasing the Kraken."

"Anyway," Logan continued assuming the propped leg pose of a storyteller, "the stewardess tells Misty there's a problem and she needs her help. Picture this, I'm standing there waiting on bended knee and I can hear her questioning what assistance she would be."

"I'm amazed you can even get down on bended knee, given how bad they are," Shelby ribbed her brother. William knew there was a reason why he liked her so much.

"Leave them alone, they get the job done." Logan affected a wounded expression. "My darling betrothed, are you going to let your future sister-in-law talk to me that way?"

"Well," Misty giggled, "she does have a point. I have to admit to a moment of anxiety myself, waiting breathlessly to see if you were ever going to be able to stand up again."

Logan gave his fiancée a lascivious wink. "At least I'll have a pretty wife to look after me in my dotage."

"And before I knew it, I'd agreed to becoming the future Mrs Logan Erikson. Now spill, Logan Erikson. Who else was in on it?" Misty's twinkling eyes were filled with love and more than a hint of frustration as she gazed at her fiancé. It went to show that opposites really did attract. William found himself seeking out Shelby, a frisson of awareness going through him when their eyes met as if she'd felt compelled to do the same.

"I've promised to take that secret to the grave with me." Logan made a show of locking his lips and throwing away the key.

Misty gave her cowboy one more narrowed-eyed glare that promised it was far from over, before sighing and turning to Shelby. "Now that we've shared our news, I want to hear all about your photoshoot."

"Um, I think it went okay," Shelby said.

"She was a success. The photographer couldn't stop raving about how much the camera loved her, and I saw the proofs—he wasn't just saying it to be nice." William frowned at the bemused smirk on Misty's face. Let her think what she wanted, it was the truth. "I have a better idea than being cooped up here sharing our news. How about we go find a quiet little bistro somewhere and eat our fill and toast our success?"

"I'd hardly call it a hardship to stay here all day," protested Shelby. "This suite is bigger than my house back home."

"I know one that's beside the most delectable patisserie." William dangled the hook in front of Shelby.

"Okay, you had me at patisserie." Shelby relented as he knew she would. She loved sweet things. "Let me go get my things then."

"We'll be waiting," said Misty. "And hurry. I think I know which one he's talking about and my mouth's watering just thinking about it."

Not needing any further urging, Shelby disappeared out the door. It was going to be fun to see Shelby's face when she saw the patisserie. He wondered if she would ever be able to pick what she wanted. He smiled to himself, making a note to get his PA to arrange for one of everything to be delivered to Shelby's suite first thing tomorrow morning.

WILLIAM COULD HAVE SWORN he was woken by a delighted shriek, but that could have just been his wishful imagination. He folded his arms behind his head and smiled, picturing Shelby's reaction to what she would have woken up to this morning. Watching her bounce between glass counters yesterday trying to make a decision had been the most fun he'd had in a long time. He'd taken women to high-end jewelers and had gotten a less enthusiastic response.

Case in point, Shelby—although thankful when he'd made several purchases for her on their shopping trip—had not shown the degree of excitement as she had faced with a choice between a pistachio macaron and the Parisian gateau.

William smiled at the thought that, with one day till her debut at Paris Fashion Week, Shelby was the only model in the city who wasn't worried about dieting.

A rumble from his belly reminded him Shelby wasn't the only one who enjoyed delicious pastries, and he reached over to order a pain au chocolat and a pot of hot chocolate. Tying a satin robe snugly about his waist, he ventured out to his rooftop terrace to enjoy the sun while he waited. William couldn't remember the last time he'd enjoyed a visit to Paris quite so much—and that was saying something since it was one of his favorite cities. Watching a male pigeon fan his tail feathers and strut in front of a potential mate, he pondered what was different.

"I'm not sure I'm all that impressed that I don't get to have my breakfast on this terrace. You know how much I love this suite." Misty sauntered in, delicate teacup in hand.

"You snooze, you lose. For someone who didn't get this suite you seem to have no issue with letting yourself in."

Misty snorted. "I swear you sounded just like Shelby then. Anyway, I thought you might want to go on a little shopping trip with me."

"Sometimes Shelbyism is the only way to accurately portray what one is feeling, and of course. Did the rodeo clown not want to go with you?"

Mystified, William watched as she stared down at her cup for a moment, a positively giddiness washing over her features. "Well, it would be bad luck if he came."

"Bad luck for him to come shopping? Bad luck for us, you mean." Taking in her glowing complexion and luminous eyes, comprehension dawned on him. "Does this mean we're going shopping for what I think we are?"

"Well, it all depends on what you think we're going shopping for." Misty tried to play it cool, but failed spectacularly, a broad grin breaking out over her face. "We decided to elope, and by that, I mean I'm getting married today."

William prided himself as a man who wasn't easily surprised, but he had to give it to his business partner—she'd outdone herself. "Like today today?"

"Yep. We got to talking last night, and we're here in the City of Love and neither of us wants a big wedding. So, um, William, would you be my Man of Honor?"

He stared at the woman glowing in front of him. Misty might never know just how much she meant to him. She'd seen in him something worthwhile all those years ago and, even when he didn't think he was worthy of her friendship, had somehow grabbed hold of him and never let go. Everything else they'd created together was icing on the cake for having her as his best friend.

"I'd be honored." He sat down and gestured for her to join him. "First order of business is for us to order some mimosas and decide what style of dress you want. I'm owed a few favors in this town, and there's no way I'm putting you in anything common."

Misty laughed as she sat down beside him. "I never doubted that for a moment." She reached over and gave his hand a squeeze. "Thanks, William, it means a lot to me."

"I know. And the clown better realize what will happen to him if he ever breaks your heart."

"I think he made a vague mention a while ago about some promises you made." Misty laughingly shook her head, the sun gleaming off her dark hair.

"Good. Then he can't say he hasn't been warned."

❧

"MOM IS GOING TO KILL YOU," Shelby predicted as she watched her brother go through his shirts before tossing them onto the bed. "I'd only be slightly less impressed if you decided to charge hell with a bucket of ice water."

Logan stared down at the shirt in his hands. "The thing is, Shelby, I messed things up with Misty so many times, I'm not taking any chances she's going to change her mind on me. I love that gal more than anything."

"Maybe, when you break the news to Mom, start with that? You know how much of a romantic she is."

"Well, as my Best Woman, maybe that falls under one of your responsibilities." Logan looked hopefully at her.

"Ah, heck no. Ain't no way on God's green earth I signed up for that. But what I did sign up for was to make sure you don't embarrass me standing up there getting hitched to the love of your life." She pushed herself off the armchair she'd been perched on. "Come on. I know someone who might be able to help. How do you feel about shiny?"

Logan scrunched his face up at her. "Like a belt buckle?"

"Oh man, you're in for a real treat. Mr Onissios is going to love you."

"Who's Mr Onissios?" Logan asked as he grabbed his hat off the bed and followed his sister.

She narrowed her eyes at him. "Don't you listen to anything Misty tells you?"

"The main things. That woman has a lot going on. She's like this multitasking army, and I'm just a simple cowboy." He placed his hat over his heart, assuming a tragic expression. "How am I meant to keep up?"

Shelby gave him a not-so-gentle sisterly shove. "That's not going to work with me." Shelby regarded him with curiosity. "So other than proposing to Misty, why do you think you're in Paris?"

"To witness your triumph as you conquer the fashion world."

She stared at him, struck speechless by what appeared to be his sincere words. "Oh."

"See? I told you I pay attention to the important things." Her brother put his hat back on his head. "Now, who's Mr Onissios?"

CHAPTER 11

*S*helby sighed dreamily over her raspberry macaron. There was something wildly romantic about eloping in Paris. Well, it would be more romantic if Billy hadn't pragmatically pointed out that it wasn't legally binding, and they would still need to have a city hall ceremony to be properly hitched. That man was such a paradox. One minute he was filling her hotel suite with the entire contents of a French patisserie and then the next minute he was all about the details. She kind of liked the contrast, it kept things interesting.

"You're not going into a diabetic coma over there, are you?" Logan asked, brushing his hair. He'd been doing it for five minutes now and that seemed like a whole heap of bother for something that was just going to have a hat mess it all up.

"No." She poked her tongue out at him.

"You know your tongue is all blue, right?"

Shelby turned to look at it in the mirror. "It must've been from the blueberry flavored thing I had."

"Aren't you the least bit suspicious of why he sent you

over all that dessert when you're meant to be skinny? At least, that's what I thought a model was supposed to look like, but what would I know? I wouldn't have said you would make a good one." Logan continued to fuss with his hair. If he kept going at this rate, Misty was going to be marrying a bald man.

"Mom always said she couldn't fatten me up, so stop picking at me." Shelby sighed again. "I think it's lovely."

Logan lowered the brush slowly and turned to look at her squarely in the face. "Do I need to have a big brother kinda talk with Billy?"

She remembered the way Billy had looked at her, the same way she'd looked at the macaron she was eating. In a room with a Russian supermodel, it was her—Shelby—who he'd looked at that way. A fluttering started in her belly, a warmth flowing through her veins. He'd looked at her like she was desirable. "Don't you go embarrassing me. There's nothing to talk to him about."

Logan twisted the brim of his hat in his hands, sending her a hard searching glance. Shelby lifted her chin defiantly. She had nothing to be ashamed off. "If you're sure. All teasing aside, Shelby, I'm your big brother and it's my job to protect you. If you set your cap for Billy, I'm just worried you're going to get hurt. You and him live very different lifestyles." Shelby's face burned, his words stinging as they hit close to home.

Suddenly all the pleasure she'd felt moments before left her. "You and Misty lived different lives before. Heck, you can't get much more different than a rodeo clown and a billionaire."

"Rodeo protection athlete," he muttered.

"I ain't one of your fancy city people, Logan. You're a rodeo clown—or at least you were until you started seeing a billionaire." She took a deep fortifying breath, trying to let go of her anger. It was her brother's wedding day, after all. "There isn't anything between me and Billy, but if there was, it wouldn't be any of your business."

Logan held up his hands in peace. "I didn't mean anything by it, I'm just being a big brother." He pulled her into a rough embrace, patting her on the back none too gently. "You're always going to be my little sister and I love you." He pulled back, tugging at his clothes. "How do I look?"

Shelby sucked on the inside of her cheek as she appraised his wedding apparel. She'd hoped Mr Onissios would be able to give her the details of someone to purchase something suitable from, only to have the designer listen to her story and take one look at her brother before muttering about handsome cowboys and the romance of Paris as he clapped his hands for his attendant.

"To help young love, it makes me feel like a young man again." When his Xandi had appeared and gave Shelby a slight smile, he quickly directed her to fetch the men's collection from last year. "I have just the thing."

Now as she stared at her brother, she was blown away by the designer's generosity. Mr Onissios had been the very model of restraint to select the garments he had, given his love of loud colors and patterns. Over a black cotton satin blend shirt, the dark navy slim fit tuxedo sat snuggly, mohair fabric giving it a wonderful sheen, and the lustrous black satin shawl lapels added a classy modernist vibe. Mr Onissios had sighed forlornly as he proclaimed his misery that he did not have a lotus silk suit to offer. But with Logan's prize buckle, cowboy boots and hat in place, her brother had somehow made it his own.

"Misty's going to get all teary-eyed when she sees you."

"Teary cause it's bad, or teary cause it's good?"

Shelby blinked. There was an edge of panic to her brother's voice. "Good." She was quick to reassure him.

"Okay." He exhaled heavily, rubbing his hands together. "Now that it's time, I'm actually getting really nervous."

Shelby stared at him for a moment before bursting out laughing. "You better not be thinking about running away. I'm too scared of Misty to let that happen. Can you imagine what she'd do when she caught you? And we both know she'd catch you."

Logan joined in the laughter, albeit with a slight edge of hysteria. "I'm scared of her too. But I'm more scared of her not being there today. Look at me, acting nervous as a fly in a glue pot." There was a vulnerability to his gaze that Shelby couldn't remember ever seeing in her brother's gaze. *He sure must love Misty a lot.*

"She spent how long being mad at you? Mom used to tell me when she talked about the two of you that it's not all that different, love and hate. Both are strong emotions."

Logan relaxed. "Yeah, I reckon back then Misty could've started an argument in an empty house."

"Logan, you have a better chance of hell freezing over than Misty not turning up."

"All right then." Shelby shuddered slightly as Logan wiped his sweaty palms on the heinously expensive fabric of his trousers. She wondered if it was dry cleanable. "Let's go get married."

"You sure you want to do this? I'm still positive you can do better than a clown." William inspected his nails closely while he waited outside the master bedroom in his suite. Misty had commandeered it since their return from their shopping trip. Too bad if he'd had plans for a nap.

"William, I have exactly the cowboy I want. Good Lord knows it took long enough to get to this point." Misty's voice sounded muffled through the door. Apparently, it had gotten to that stage of getting ready. Thankfully the makeup artist, Suzie, was on hand to help.

"A Paris elopement is so romantic," cooed Suzie.

"And practical. It still gives Misty a get out of jail free card if she gets back to the States and comes to her senses. Only two witnesses, nothing legally binding. Misty always was a clever clogs." Bored, William strode to the glass doors and peered outside. Catching himself in the reflection, he paused to appraise his appearance. To an outsider it might have come across as vain, but William liked to have every detail taken care of. His cream linen suit complemented his pale lemon shirt perfectly, the top two buttons undone. The tan loafers—sans socks, of course—just the right color to not abruptly cut off the line of his leg. It screamed casual as only the wealthy could do.

A movement behind him drew his attention away from himself. Turning slowly, he openly studied the vision in front of him. The mermaid cut ivory gown showcased Misty's curves in all the right ways. No doubt the clown would be drooling when he saw her. The aged ivory lace stomacher emphasized an already slender waist into nothing. He'd had to pull in a few favors to get this gown for his best friend, but seeing her standing there, glowing, he knew he'd have walked over hot coals if that's what it would have taken.

"Logan's not going to be able to string a sentence together, let alone be able to say 'I do,'" he drily noted.

"I think a grunt is enough in a pinch." Misty gave a slow twirl. "So, I pass inspection?"

"Like I'd have picked out something for you that wouldn't." An odd feeling settled over him. He and Misty had met when they were kids trying to pretend they were adults. But now it suddenly hit him that they were grown up and his best friend was getting married. "Your cowboy better know how lucky he is," he growled gruffly, keenly aware of his loneliness.

Misty winked at him. "I make sure to remind him every day." Somehow, intuitively, understanding shone in her eyes, and she moved closer, reaching out to clasp his hands. "Looks like you're going to be best friends with an old married lady."

"Does this mean I'm the one of us who ends up with the twelve cats?"

"Hardly. You wouldn't stand for all the cat fur." She smiled softly at him. "But I want you to promise me that you will open yourself to the prospect of letting love into your life. I'd hate for you to miss out on it because you're too scared of letting someone get close to you. Not every marriage is like your parents'."

Her words aroused old fears, memories that still taunted him after all these years. "Well, thank goodness for that."

Misty didn't release his hands. "Promise me, William."

Knowing she could be like a dog with a bone, he relented. After all, it was her wedding day. "I promise." An image of a smiling fresh-faced Shelby forced its way into his mind as he said the words.

"Good. Now let's go make sure Shelby has gotten Logan to the church on time." The gleam of determination in Misty's eyes was so fierce that, for a moment, he almost felt sorry for the clown. Almost.

Later after a ceremony that might've only had the two of them for all the attention Misty and Logan paid anyone else, William found himself stepping outside for a moment of fresh air. Inside the lovebirds continued to only have eyes for each other as they celebrated their wedding day over dinner. Being around so much love made the loneliness settle like a canker in his heart. Sighing, he leaned against the rail of the terrace.

"You look lower than a gopher hole." Despite his mood, Shelby's words made his lips twitch. He dared anyone to not feel better when she was around. He took in the dress she was wearing, the one he'd bought her earlier in the week. Had it only been a couple of days? He couldn't imagine what his days had been like before Shelby had been around to fill them. She jerked her thumb back inside. "Unlike those two making moon-eyes at each other."

"It's positively sickening," he agreed. "I usually make it a practice to not attend weddings, and yet, I've been to two in the past year all thanks to that lady inside." A thought suddenly struck him, and he gave a half smile. "And you've been beside me for both of them."

Shelby blinked at him. "That's right. I hadn't really thought of that before."

He raised his drink to her in toast. "We may as well make it official. It appears that you are henceforth to be my wedding companion."

"Except you don't normally attend any." She seemed a little sad, the sparkle a little dimmer than usual.

"But if I do, you're my girl."

"Why don't you go to weddings?" Intense curiosity overcame the sadness in her expression.

"I don't believe in marriage. My parents cured me of that particular flight of fancy, and then once I became this eligible billionaire bachelor you see standing before you, well, everyone wanted to invite me to their weddings to try to marry me to their second cousin twice removed, of course."

"Of course," Shelby murmured. "I love weddings. Seeing people in love and happy—and of course, there's dancing and cake." She looked over her shoulder back inside. "They are going to give us cake, right?"

William chuckled and he reached out to give Shelby's hand a squeeze. He felt a curious swooping pull deep in his stomach. Somehow touching her was both comforting and nerve-tingling at the same time. "If they don't give you cake, I'll get you some," he promised.

Her face lit up, making him feel like he'd just promised her the Empire State Building. "I'm going to hold you to that."

"I wouldn't have it any other way." Standing there with his cowgirl, the moon shining above them in a clear, inky black Parisian night sky, he knew he'd never spoken truer words.

CHAPTER 12

*W*omen in various stages of undress flitted around like exotic, statuesque butterflies. Standing in the epicenter of it all, Shelby couldn't help feeling like a drab little moth. A moth that wanted to be anywhere but here with the beautiful people who stared at her and whispered between themselves. A vortex of hyperventilating panic threatened to grab hold of her.

Blinking rapidly, she miserably looked down at her feet, wanting to be back home where she belonged, covered in grease and hidden under the hood of a car.

"Ladies, gather around." Spying Shelby, Mr Onissios swooped in, taking hold of her hand. "This, ladies, is my muse." He brought her hand to his lips and kissed it. "Every garment you wear today has been inspired by her."

If looks could kill, she'd be dead, judging from the way Annika glared at her as she whispered to the gorgeous ebony-skinned model beside her. Her friend giggled at whatever was said. If ever there was a time for a hole to suddenly appear in the ground, now was definitely it. Shelby tried to smile, but she knew it was too forced and probably looked more like a grimace. She pressed her lips together, desperately feeling like she wanted to vomit.

With a supreme act of self-control, Shelby blinked back the tears that trembled on her eyelids, conscious of the glares, side glances and snide whispers as the models dispersed back to whatever it was they did backstage. Shelby wasn't exactly sure what that was yet. She might not feel like she belonged here, but she sure as heck wasn't going to let these women make her feel that way. Heck, they made a hornet look cuddly.

"Suzie," Mr Onissios called, waving to the makeup artist. Shelby stared at the lavender mohawk the woman now wore. It was startling.

"Yo, Mr O," she said as she bounced over, a ball of pure energy apparently fueled by sugar.

"It is because I love you that I let you call me that. If it were anyone else..." the designer threatened gruffly, a fond gleam in his eye.

"I know, Mr O, with power comes great responsibility. Hey, Shelby, I saw some more of your pictures and they are AMAZING." Suzie finished in a sing song voice. "Mr O, you want me to get started on her makeup?"

"Yes." Mr Onissios focused on Shelby. "Today you are no longer just my muse, which is honor enough," he said humbly. "Today you become a star." He fanned his hands out in front of him as if her name would be in lights. Shelby wasn't sure if she remembered signing up to be a star. Texas was beginning to feel a long way away. "Now, go with Suzie and let her work her magic."

Suzie gave Shelby a jaunty grin. "I don't need magic when I have a canvas this good to work on. Come on, I'll show you where I want you to sit." Shelby kept her gaze laser-focused on the back of the makeup artist as they made their way through the models. "Sit here, please." Suzie pointed to her workstation. "Normally you would go from me to a hair-stylist, and then over there"—she waved to rows of clothing racks—"would be where your outfits would be. Now, because William was worried you might get a bit daunted by all this backstage stuff, he suggested to Mr O that maybe it might be better just to keep you in one little area. Easier to remember and all that."

If Billy had been backstage, Shelby would have kissed him —no maybe about it. He really did try to think of everything. A warm glow filled her that he might think she was special enough to make sure she was okay on her big day. "It really would make it easier."

"Now, this woman here"—Suzie pointed to a tall silver-haired woman, her hair color not so much a symbol of age as her sophistication hovering in the background—"her name is Mimi, and what she doesn't know about fashion shows isn't worth knowing. She's going to be your dresser today."

Shelby twisted in her chair and waved at the glorious Mimi. "Hi, um, but what does a dresser do?" She tried not to slump down in her chair at revealing her ignorance.

"It is exactly what the name suggests. I am going to dress you." Her Italian accent lent a wonderful cadence to her words as she spoke.

"I don't know that I need help dressing, I've been doing it myself for quite a while now." Shelby's face flamed. Heck, the last person to help her had been her mom when she was four!

Mimi and Suzi laughed at her indignation. "But here you need to get changed into elaborate outfits complete with accessories in a matter of minutes," Suzie pointed out, leaving Shelby feeling foolish. "Models always have dressers backstage, and every model wants Mimi." Suzie picked up her brushes pouch, ready to set to work on Shelby. "You should've heard Annika screech when she found out she wasn't getting her." She winked impishly at Mimi. "You didn't seem too upset not to have to deal with her tantrums."

"That one has the temperament of a hormonal badger," Mimi sagely replied. Apparently, the woman didn't ruffle easily.

"Oh great, one more reason for her and the others to hate me." Shelby sighed. Billy might as well have painted a target on her back. She began to pick at her ragged cuticle.

Mimi waved her hand dismissively. "The true greats do not bother to lower themselves to jealousy. Instead they seek to help lift up those coming through behind them. I also find that models tend to be irritable when they are hungry, and most of these girls haven't eaten three full meals a day for quite some time." Shelby gauged wisdom in the older woman's words.

"You should listen to Mimi. She knows what she's talking about. Now, close your eyes," Suzie instructed.

Obeying, she tried to steady the nerves coursing through her with each beat of her heart. She was a mechanic from Texas who actually considered dressing up the difference between her work jeans and her good jeans. What was she doing here? And then she thought of those smiling faces again—she couldn't let them down. She would do it for them and a certain handsome billionaire who just so happened to believe she could do it, too.

Faster than small town gossip, Shelby found herself standing at the edge of the backstage curtain at the head of a snaking, compacted line of models. Beside her, a no-nonsense man stood, mic'd up and device in hand.

"Walk to the end, pause, stare out so the photographers can get a good photo, turn, walk back, repeat," she muttered to herself like a mantra. Shelby swallowed hard, trying not to give in to paralyzing stage fright.

"Listen to her." Annika snickered from behind her. "I

don't know what Mr Onissios was thinking letting her open the show." High-pitched giggles responded. Shelby wasn't sure from who, but there was no way she was going to turn around to find out. With renewed humiliation, she stared ahead.

"And cue the music," the man beside her said. "And three-two-one, Shelby, you're good to go."

Taking a deep breath, Shelby forced her frozen limbs into motion, fearful that if she didn't do it immediately, they were going to have to push her out onto the stage. The lights were blindingly white, allowing her only glimpses of those in the front row. Head held high, she found herself naturally stepping to the beat of the music, the fabric of her dress whispering as it swished with each exaggerated stride she took. From the corner of her eyes, she could see Misty and Logan, her brother's hand resting possessively on his wife's leg. They were leaving for their honeymoon to Portofino as soon as the show was over. Apparently, that wasn't quick enough for Logan. Shelby's lips twitched as he brought his free hand to his mouth and let out an ear-piercing whistle.

Billy gave a nod of approval, his smile sending warm shivers down her spine. She was doing it. No, she was more than doing it. She was doing brilliantly—even Billy thought so. Shelby got to the end and struck a pose, the flash of the cameras making her feel like she was confronting a strobe light. Then, with a haughty toss of her head—gosh, she was enjoying pretending to be a model—she spun on her heel and began to make her way back up the catwalk. Several models behind, Annika narrowed her eyes as she saw her make her way back to the applause of the crowd. *How do you like them apples, Annika?* Nothing was going to stop the buzz Shelby had going on.

It took a few more strides to realize that if one of them didn't change their course, they would collide, and if Shelby went anymore to the side, she was liable to fall off. She glared back at Annika. She wasn't going to be intimidated—not out here. But the Russian only continued her game of catwalk chicken. Shelby held her breath, waiting for the moment of impact, steeling herself. At the last moment, Annika changed her course minutely, putting Shelby slightly off balance in her sky-high heels.

Sweet relief trickled through her. Even Annika wouldn't dare pull a stunt like that—not out here. And then it happened. A not-so-subtle shoulder shove as the other model went past her, sending her flying off the side of the runway. Stunned, Shelby could only lay winded as unfamiliar faces peered down at her before raucous laughter rippled through the crowd. Mortified, she crawled to her feet, ungainly in her heels, and slung away backstage to hide.

But Mimi wouldn't allow her to escape so easily, wiping the tears away as she pulled the dress from her only to replace it with a mini. "Shelby, I don't care what happened out there. You still have another look to do, and there's no way you're going to miss it on my watch. As long as you can still walk, you're going to stiffen that lip and get back out there." For the second time that evening, Shelby was on the receiving end of a not-so-subtle shove.

Tears stung her eyes at the memory of what had just happened. Mortified, she couldn't bring herself to look at Billy. And then through the cloud of her misery she heard a noise. A slow steady clap—just the one person. Eyes wide, she saw her brother standing in his place, and then Billy took up the beat, then Misty standing beside him, shoulder to shoulder in support of her. And then more—one by one until the entire crowd was on its feet, encouraging her journey. Tears still threatened, but they were no longer ones of humiliation.

Later as she found a moment of peace in a bathroom

cubicle, she quietly cried, releasing all the pent-up emotions of the day, her body aching from her tumble.

The sound of the door swinging open carried in several voices. "Oh my goodness, when Mr Onissios said she was the inspiration for his collection, I almost died," an unfamiliar woman said. "Well, I didn't know this collection was for the unwashed masses. If I'd known, I wouldn't have cheapened my brand and walked his show. I'm going to tell my agency that I'm not happy. What about you, Annika?"

"Well, it's obvious she's a charity case. After all, I heard her brother is dating the CEO or something," the Russian replied. *Married to the CEO. Get it right!* "Like how she talks. I can't decide if she lives in a trailer or a barn." As high-pitched giggles echoed about, Shelby's humiliation slowly turned to anger. With a fire in her belly, she stood. She was going to give these girls a piece of her mind. "I'll have to ask William on our next date." Shelby's whole world came crashing down around her, a dull ring sounding in her ears as her legs collapsed and she sunk back down to the toilet seat.

"Didn't you guys break up?" asked another voice.

An awkward silence sounded outside. "We didn't break up." Annika's voice was cutting. "It's just that I'm super busy and he's super busy. We still catch up all the time and he's still very attentive when we do, if you know what I mean." Her words were just more vinegar to Shelby's open wounds. "Now, there's an afterparty I don't intend on missing."

"Especially with billionaire lover boy waiting for you." One of Annika's cronies giggled.

Clicking heels and then the door slammed shut behind them, leaving Shelby to her misery. Hot tears scalded her face as she cried silently. She didn't want to believe the bond she'd felt growing between them had been nothing more than something to pass the time till Annika wasn't busy. No, Billy wasn't like that. *He's a billionaire. He can have anything he wants at the click of his fingers. Why wouldn't he want a Russian supermodel?* whispered her tortured mind.

Breaking completely, she ran from the bathroom. She needed her mom.

~

SEEING Shelby own that catwalk was one of the proudest days of William's life. She'd looked like an Amazonian Queen gracing them with her presence. When she'd tumbled from the runway, he'd been out of his seat before he'd had time to think, his heart in his mouth. William was not a man prone to violence. Not once had he raised his fists back at his father in all those years of beatings, even when he'd grown bigger than him. As a man, he'd found his cutting tongue a much more effective weapon than any degree of brutality.

But when the crowd had started to laugh at Shelby, he'd been ready to knock teeth in. The urge had been primal and instinctive. But she'd managed to scramble to her feet and was gone by the time he'd reached where she'd landed. And then she'd appeared again in a change of outfits, composed, beautiful, and he'd never wanted to hug someone so much in his whole life, especially knowing how she must have felt but had hidden.

Actually, as soon as William found Shelby, he was going to wrap her up in a hug so tight and tell her exactly how proud he was of her. Scanning the chaotic backstage dressing area, he was at a loss to find her. Seeing Suzie, he waved her over. "Have you seen Shelby?"

Suzie gave a shrug, shaking her head. "Not since Mimi changed her out of her last outfit. Maybe she was so amped up that she took off straight to the afterparty."

William stepped back slightly as he eyed her mohawk. If she wasn't careful, she was liable to take someone's eye out.

He could imagine what it must feel like to have all that energy coursing through one's body after a performance like that. "Do you know if she was okay after her fall?"

"She already had bruises coming up on her knees and hips, but she said she was fine. I didn't see it myself and she didn't say much, but what happened?"

"One minute she was owning it up there and then when Annika went past, she just went down." A niggling suspicion itched at the back of his mind. *Could it really just be a coincidence that it had happened just as Annika went by?* The need to find Shelby intensified. "If you see Shelby, can you let her know that I'm going to the afterparty to try to find her?"

"Shall do."

A short stroll—or this case, a forced march—down the Champs-Élysées and the afterparty was pulsing, strobe lights flashing, and the space filled to capacity with drunk beautiful people. Having had little to eat, the first glass of champagne always seemed to make models tipsy. Pushing his way through the dance floor to get to the raised DJ's booth for a better vantage, William was the victim of loose elbows and feet thrown about in reckless abandon. Sourly, he noted that Annika had commandeered the raised platform to better display her dance moves, sheathed in skintight leather and surrounded by her fawning friends. The outfit made her look gaunt. *Shelby better appreciate him throwing himself in the lions' den for her.*

"William, I knew you would come find me." Annika threw her arms dramatically around him, making a show of pressing against his body. Sternly, he took her by the arms and pulled her away from him. "William, why are you such a party-pooper tonight? That little farm girl isn't around, so you don't have to act like we aren't a thing."

Okay, Shelby wasn't here, but where? Relieved, William began to edge away, preparing to leave. He paused on the cusp and looked back at the pouting Russian. "Oh, and Annika, we were never a thing. We had a few dates that we both enjoyed and that was it, nothing more. I know you weren't exactly heartbroken, given all the guys the media have pictures of you draping yourself over."

The models close to Annika snickered. William had to shake his head at the dog-eat-dog attitude. Shelby really was too good to even share air with this crowd. They were filled with insecurities and emptiness—how he used to feel, he realized, until Shelby had come and filled all that dark loneliness with light. There was only one other place he could think of that she might be. Stepping off the dais, he plunged into the crowd to find her.

Twenty minutes later, perspiring and breathing hard, William had to laugh at the state he'd gotten himself into. Normally there was no way he'd let anyone see him at less than perfection. Raising his hand, he knocked on the Coco Chanel suite door. Silence. He knocked again. Silence again.

"Shelby, I know you're in there."

"No, I'm not." William smiled at the little girl petulance in her voice.

"Okay, well, whoever this is that isn't Shelby, do you think she might come to the door so I don't have to yell everything?"

He found himself leaning in, trying to catch any trace of movement. The lock clicked loudly in his ear and, with a jerk of surprise, he straightened. Shelby's face had been scrubbed clean of the makeup and her hair pulled back into a ponytail. Gone was the fabulous couture, now she was in sweats. Her nose looked red and there was a pallor to her cheeks. *Had she been more hurt than they'd realized when she'd fallen?*

"Do you need me to take you to the hospital?"

Shelby blinked at him. "What?"

Maybe she'd gotten concussed. "Where does it hurt?"

"Everywhere. I feel like a Mack truck ran me over, but I don't need to go to the hospital."

Some of his worry evaporated, leaving only confusion. "Then why are you here and not celebrating?"

"I did the job you and Misty wanted me to do, and now I'm done." She crossed her arms over her chest, her expression hard. "You know, I was happy and comfortable in my own skin, being little old me. Was it all some kind of joke to you?" Her voice trembled. "But you know what? When I took away the false eyelashes and those fancy clothes, I'm still me, and I like me." Her expression hardened. "But if I take away all your money and all the fancy from you, would you even know who you were anymore?"

William was caught off-guard by the sudden attack. *What had changed?* His defenses snapped back into place. This was why—with the exception of Misty—he never let anyone get close. They were just looking for ways to hurt him. He'd thought Shelby was different from the rest, but apparently, she wasn't.

"Be ready to leave in the morning. We'll be stopping at my private island for a few days and then you'll never have to see me again." He wondered why the idea hurt so much.

CHAPTER 13

*W*ith the exception of the trip to Myanmar and Paris, Shelby had been outside of the United States a grand total of one time and that had been to Mexico for Spring Break. Watching the island rise out of the turquoise water of the Pacific Ocean, she'd never seen anything quite so breathtaking in her entire life. From her perch at the bow of the speed boat, she could only stare in awe as the wind whipped her hair about her face in a frenzy. When they'd boarded Misty's plane, she'd assumed they would land somewhere on the island. But the small open-aired airport they'd disembarked at had only been her first taste of Fiji. Skimming across the sea on a luxury boat, salt-water spray kissing her skin, had been an unexpected treat. A soothing balm to the angry words she'd flung at Billy in a moment of hurt.

For his part, Billy had spoken politely—if distantly—since then, and each time she felt the gulf widen between them. A few days on this island paradise and then this magical experience she'd shared with him would be over. Spying a wharf jutting out from the protected lagoon side of the island, she saw a lone figure standing on the end to greet them. Shelby shielded her eyes. It looked like a woman.

"That will be the new caregiver." She hadn't heard Billy join her.

"Have you met her before?"

"No, this is actually the first time I've visited the island since I purchased it. I had an agent arrange to hire one for me." Shelby couldn't imagine owning paradise and not having seen it till now. The boat began to slow as it lined up its moorings, coasting the final distance until it made contact with a jolt. A crew member threw a line to the woman and Shelby watched fascinated as she expertly secured it.

"Welcome to Vunde Waitui," the woman greeted them as they joined her on the pier. On closer inspection, the woman was older than she'd expected, her skin weathered by the elements to give her deep crinkles around her mouth and dark eyes. "I'm Maura." She extended her hand, eyes searching Billy's face intently.

He took her proffered hand. "I'm William, and this is Shelby. How have you been getting on here?"

When she smiled, all the lines on her face danced to life. "Just fine. It's a beautiful place and hasn't caused me one ounce of trouble." Maura looked past them to the luggage that was being placed on the wharf. "Can you take them to the master suite?" she directed.

Shelby colored at the assumption. "No, um." She shook her head quickly.

"Please take my luggage to the master suite and Shelby's to the guest suite," Billy said, gazing at the villa in the distance. "I think I'll familiarize myself with the lay of everything and join you both later for sunset drinks." Having made his mind up, he strode decisively off, leaving Shelby and Maura to stare at his departing back.

"I'm sorry, I shouldn't have assumed," Maura said after a moment. "It's just that the two of you seemed … together?"

Shelby wanted to laugh, considering they'd never been so far apart and, given the disagreements they'd had over the course of knowing each other, that was really saying something. A heaviness centered in her chest. She missed him. "At best, for a brief, happy moment we were friends."

Maura gave her a searching look. "I see."

Shelby didn't think she did. After all, how could she if Shelby didn't?

She gaped at the villa as Maura showed her through, explaining that it had been built in the style of a Fijian Bure. Shelby could only nod as her head swiveled about. The high-pitched thatched roof had exposed carved timber rafters on the ceiling. Fans lazily turned, swirling the heavy air about, and brightly colored tropical flowers floated languidly in enormous water-filled carved stone bowls. Maura threw open a carved double door.

"This will be your room for your stay. Although it's not the master, I'm sure you'll have no complaints."

The older woman gave her a knowing smile, waiting for her to take in her accommodation. Floor-to-ceiling windows gave an uninterrupted view of the infinity pool directly outside and the azure pacific beyond it. Coconut and banana trees fringed the vista. Shelby pulled her overwhelmed eyes to take in the interior. Warm timbers, crisp whites and stone accents filled a room that was larger than her house back in Texas.

"Wow."

Maura chuckled. "I couldn't say it better myself. The wardrobe has a selection of kaftans and sarongs—all brand new, I promise. They've been made by some of the local women. Please avail yourself of them if you wish." She raised a brow at Shelby's jeans. "In case you find denim is too hot for island life."

Laughing, Shelby looked down at her jeans and cowboy boots. "You can take the cowgirl out of Texas."

"I'll leave you to settle in. If there's anything you need, please dial one on the phone and it will connect you straight through to me. Otherwise, I will arrange a kava ceremony to take place at six-thirty this evening to welcome you and William to the island." With a final warm smile, Maura left Shelby to admire her tropical surroundings.

IT HAD ONLY TAKEN William a few minutes shy of an hour to walk the entire island, including long dramatic pauses looking off into the Pacific. Seeing the villa in the distance, he glumly sat down on a large rocky outcrop. Where had it all gone wrong? He could have sworn there was something between him and Shelby, and then she'd turned on him. Of course, he knew who he was. He was William Irvine, one of the youngest self-made billionaires in history. Idly, he picked up a shell, tracing the rough ridges with his index finger. What would happen if he really did lose it all? He'd pulled himself up by his bootstraps before and, if he had to, he could do it all over again.

"Excuse me, William?" Maura appeared, uncertainty dancing across her face. Obviously, she found it unsettling to have her new boss appear and then immediately disappear to sulk.

"Yes, Maura?" William lopped the shell at the gently lapping waves.

"I've arranged for the chief from the local village on the neighboring island to come and hold a kava ceremony. He'll be ready to start in twenty minutes."

"I don't remember asking you to organize one."

"I know, and I apologize for taking the liberty." She wrung her hands. "But it is traditionally something that takes place."

William sighed. Maura had obviously been trying to do what she thought was best. "What do I need to do?"

"Not much. Be there, do what he tells you. Oh, and give him this." She held out a root.

"What is that?"

"It's the root of the yaqona. It's what the kava is made from. By giving it to the chief, it will show that you know the proper etiquette for the ceremony."

"Even if I don't?"

She smiled warmly at him. "Even if you don't."

"Well, I guess I'd better not keep him waiting." William stood and brushed the sand from the seat of his pants. "Lead the way."

With a sure stride, Maura led him to where a palm frond mat had been laid out, a small group gathered around it. "Bula," she greeted them, enthusiastic bulas ringing in response. "This is William. He is the new owner of the island. And this"—she continued, spying Shelby hesitantly approaching the group—"is Shelby. That's everyone."

The man who, judging by the reverence the others gave him, was the leader sat down and indicated for them to form a circle around him. "Have either of you ever participated in a kava ceremony?"

"No," Shelby said, settling her kaftan around her. *When did she get a kaftan?* "I've never heard of it."

"I'm in the same boat as Shelby." William's heart beat a little faster at the grateful smile she sent his way. "However, I believe this is for you." He held out the root Maura had given him.

The chief's teeth flashed brightly as he smiled. "Thank

you. First, we will prepare it." He took a large communal bowl and placed it in front of him. "This is the tanoa bowl." He began to pound the root until it was pulverized. Taking the pulp and placing it into a cloth sack, he mixed it with water. The end result was a brownish liquid that reminded William of muddy water. He took a cup and held it over the bowl. "I will show you how it is done."

He filled it to the brim and offered it to Maura. William watched bemused as she clapped once and yelled "Bula!" before, with a single gulp, she downed it. He wondered if it tasted as bad as it looked. She then clapped three times before yelling "Maca!" Maura smiled at him. "Now it's your turn."

She handed the cup back to the chief, who looked expectantly at William. "High tide or low tide?"

William stared at the chief, aware that he looked like a simpleton. "I'm sorry, what?"

"He means do you want a full cup or half cup?" Maura helpfully supplied.

"A little bit?" William hedged, it was better to get a little down than vomit over the chief.

"No wet sand here. I give you high tide," the chief declared, filling the cup to the brim and holding it expectantly out to William.

William sent his stomach a stern warning as he clapped his hands and shouted the obligatory "Bula!", throwing the contents down his throat before his body went into outright revolt. He quickly swallowed and clapped his hands three times. "Maca!"

Relieved, he handed the cup back. It had a distinctly earthy flavor, and he was pretty confident that even devotees of the drink would never call it smooth. William became aware of a pleasant, numb feeling around his mouth, spreading to his lips and tongue. A sense of calm and serenity flowed through him as he watched Shelby repeat the process he'd just completed. There was a glow to her tonight. Island life suited her.

She wiped her mouth on the sleeve of her kaftan. "Thank you. That's, um, the best kava I've ever tasted." Why hadn't he thought to say something like that?

The chief beamed his appreciation at her and, with the cup having completed its journey around the circle and returned to his hands, he made his farewells and departed with his companions.

"Did it taste like muddy water strained through gym socks to you?" Shelby asked, touching her lips experimentally with a fingertip.

"Yes." William laughed. "But you're the one who came up with the best compliment. You did tell him at the beginning that you'd never had any before though."

Shelby's eyes grew round with horror. "Oh no! I forgot. Do you think I offended him?"

"I'm sure he took it in the spirit it was given." Maura was quick to reassure her.

"It certainly has some interesting side effects." William made some fish faces with his lips.

Shelby's laughter was infectious, and he freely joined her. "I like it when you're like this," she said, mirth dancing in her eyes.

"When I drink kava? Because I'm not sure it's something I can commit to."

She giggled again. "No, it's like you're not worried about trying to impress anyone."

William smirked at her. "Then I'll have to try harder, because I've been trying to impress you since we left Texas."

"Billy, about what I said in Paris." Shelby's eyes were luminous as she worried her bottom lip with her teeth.

"It's okay." He surprised himself with the peace that

wrapped itself around him. *It really was okay.* "Can we agree to go back to before whatever it was that happened?"

She managed a tremulous smile. "I'd like that. I really would." William was drowning in beautiful pale blue eyes and the need to kiss that mouth.

Maura cleared her throat. *Why was she still here?* "There's a reason the Fijians often serve kava to settle arguments or make peace. If you'll excuse me, it's time for me to prepare dinner."

William watched her go. Now he had Shelby all to himself. A soft snore sounded from behind him. Twisting back around, he found the object of his desire asleep on her side. Sighing, he rose and gathered her tightly to her chest. There was still the most marvelous peace cocooned around him, such that all he could do was smile tenderly down at the woman in his arms. Best get Sleeping Beauty to bed.

CHAPTER 14

Some people need at least eight hours of sleep to feel human. William had always managed on the bare minimum and had seen it as a challenge to fight against. Waking up feeling refreshed, he could only marvel at how luxurious it felt to be free of exhaustion. Sure, the bed was comfortable, but it didn't matter where he slept, they all were. The clean bed linen and of the finest quality certainly helped. The gentle rhythm of the waves, unstoppable as they slowly eroded and remolded the shore in a continuous dance as old as time had been soothing. Puzzled at why he'd slept so well, he padded to the shower. And it hit him. The kava ceremony and Shelby. One was easy to implement. He was pretty sure he could find a way to get kava capsules that would bypass the muddy water taste. But Shelby—what to do about her?

He still wasn't sure what had happened in Paris. Shelby had tried last night to tell him, and in his blissed-out state, he'd stopped her. Now he was having major regrets about that. Whistling, he began to lather up. It didn't matter. One way or another, he was going to get back to how things had been with Shelby, and this time it was going to go much better than almost kissing. Deep down in his soul he felt the pull of the island. Maybe Shelby felt the same.

"Argh!" he bellowed as the steamy water turned frigid, moments before spluttering and stopping completely. William fumbled with the tap, turning it off and on again. Maybe water was like a computer and all it needed was a reboot. Getting no joy, he wrapped his towel around his waist and marched off in search of his caretaker.

Shelby stared bemused at him, the slice of mango she'd been about to take a bite from raised halfway to her mouth. Suddenly, she didn't seem to know where to look, a suspicious smothered coughing fit overcoming her. "Um, is this island life, too?"

"Not the type I'm familiar with." Maura raised a brow at him. "I believe you've forgotten something, young man." She sounded for all the world like a mother about to tell him off.

"Yeah, like the water. What did you do?" William folded his arms before quickly abandoning the stance as his towel threatened to loosen. He clutched it tightly in one hand and continued to glare at the amused women.

"There's some dripping on my clean floor," Maura pointed out.

"If you go turn on a tap, I bet you'll find that's all there is," William said through gritted teeth. Frowning thoughtfully at him, Maura went to the sink and turned the tap, giving a surprised *humph* when nothing happened. "I told you so."

"Well, I guess there's something wrong with the pump then," Maura said. "I'll call someone and organize for them to come out and look at it."

"Do you have tools on the island?" Shelby asked, putting her mango down and wiping her hands.

"Yes, and some spare parts the old owners left," Maura said. "The island is fully self-sufficient. We run solar and wind turbines that charge batteries, and harvest our own water. Most things I can fix, but pumps and motors are things I stay well away from."

"It's a good thing that's what I'm good at then." Shelby rubbed her hands together enthusiastically. "If you tell me where the tools are stored, I'll go see what needs doing."

"If you follow that path"—Maura pointed outside the door—"it will lead you to the workshop and everything you should need."

"Great." Whistling a happy tune to herself, Shelby went in search of the aforementioned workshop.

Maura looked at the dripping William. "Are you still standing there?'

Chastised, he slunk back to his rooms to get changed.

When he found Shelby, she had the pump—or at least what he assumed was the pump—pulled apart. For all he knew, it could've been part of a boat. Already she had a spot of grease on her cheek and a smile on her face. She'd never looked more beautiful to him.

"If you're going to stand there staring at me, best make yourself useful and hand me that shifter," she said without glancing from her work. His hand hovered over the collection of tools in front of him. *Maybe it was this one?* William closed in on it. "Nope."

"Hey, you didn't even look up." He detested feeling foolish, but somehow it didn't feel like she was mocking him, just joining him in on the joke.

"Didn't have to. It's the large silver one." Triumphantly, he grabbed it and passed it to her.

"Do you know why it isn't working?" He peered over her shoulder. His lips twitched as he wondered why he even bothered—it wasn't like he knew what he was looking for.

"Well, it seems like ants have decided to make a home in the motor and they've shorted it out. I'm cleaning them all out and giving it a spray and then I'll put it all back together and we'll give it a try." She blew into a part before setting it back down. "Pliers."

Those he knew. He collected them and with a flourish handed them over to her expectant hand. William waited for her to acknowledge his competence, but she continued with her work. Deflated, he sat down, waiting for her next request. And so it went on for the better part of several hours. She began to explain what she was doing and why, having decided to take the opportunity to check that everything was in working order. As she put it, she didn't want to go to all the trouble of putting it back together only to have to pull it apart in a few days when something else went wrong. He surprised himself with enjoying it all immensely.

Shelby secured the last bolt and handed him the wrench. "You're not that bad—well, once you figured out which tool was which. If this billionaire thing doesn't work out for you, I might even consider taking you on as my apprentice."

He tipped an imaginary hat at her. "Why, thank you for your kind words, ma'am."

Shelby giggled as she wiped the sweat from her brow, leaving another dirt mark on her face. "Was that the first time you've ever worked with your hands like that?"

"My dad worked construction." William wasn't sure why he told her that. He scowled as he began to pack the tools away.

"You don't really talk about him."

"That's because there's nothing to tell. He deserves nothing but bad things to happen to him, and if I'm really lucky, I'll never hear anything but that about him." Shelby rocked back on her heels as if shocked by the venom he knew laced each word. "You see, I wasn't man enough for him, cause I was a nerd and liked computers." Bitterness pulled his mouth into a sour smile. "He'd probably have loved you. Thought you were a better man than me."

"And I hate him for treating you like that." His heart twitched at her proud loyalty.

"I left home as soon as I could and never looked back." William twisted the screwdriver around in his hands. "I don't even know if he's still alive, and that's fine with me. He was a horrible, abusive man with no redeeming qualities. I never wanted to be like him, and I made sure I wasn't." Something clicked in his mind. "Maybe that's why I said what I did to you."

Shelby's face scrunched. "You're going to have to narrow it down."

He laughed ruefully. "I've put my foot in it a few times, haven't I? About getting a better life than what you have before I even knew what your life was like. You see, how I am now—what the money can get me—I enjoy that a whole lot. I guess maybe I wanted that for you too. It was arrogant of me."

She narrowed her eyes at him. "Is that a sincere apology I hear from you, William Irvine?"

"It truly is, Shelby Erikson. But in my own way, I was trying to care—and I do care, you know. Trust me, you're more than perfect as you are."

"It didn't feel that way being surrounded by all those beautiful women." A sad acceptance took the glow from her eyes as she shrugged. "I've always been one of the guys. It felt beyond strange to have people comment solely on how I looked. It was uncomfortable, like they were making fun of me. And then, of course, I found out that the models were actually making fun of me."

William's mood veered sharply to anger. "Why would they make fun of you? Give me their names." There was a silky promise of threat to his soft words.

"Well, for years it was because of how I looked. I know what I see in the mirror, I'm not stupid or blind. I'm not beautiful. I'm too tall, too plain, my mouth too wide, and I'm normally okay with that. I have other skills and I'm a nice person, dang it. But back in Paris, none of that mattered as much."

A fierce emotion that William couldn't name choked him. He could guess who some of the culprits were, but as soon as he had names, he was going to make some phone calls. Life was about to get a lot tougher for some of them. "I've been around a lot of beautiful women."

"Yeah, I know. Your girlfriend made sure I knew," she interrupted quietly.

William frowned at her. "What girlfriend?"

She raised her brows sky high. "Um, Annika?"

"Trust me, that one has never been my girlfriend. My taste leans to something a little different." *Like cowboy boots and engine grease.* "But I think you'll agree I'm qualified to make this comment. You're right, you're not like them." Her face fell and she began to blink rapidly. Tenderly, he raised her face to stare into her tear-filled eyes. "You're the most beautiful woman I've ever had the pleasure—no, the honor—of meeting, let alone get to know. You glow from within with something so pure and special it's blinding. Those other women are just fake carbon copies of each other. The camera is what fills them with substance for that brief moment and then, once the flash is gone, they're back to being empty again. Don't be like them, be you."

Her compelling eyes riveted William to the spot. His heart began hammering foolishly. Shelby was a revelation to him. In one smooth motion, she was in his arms, and with that movement, the last thread of his self-control snapped. His mouth covered hers hungrily, and male satisfaction surged through him as she returned his kiss passionately, her body perfectly molded to his like two halves of a whole. The missing piece to the hole in his heart.

∿

HER LIPS FELT like that time she'd tried a tingling lip balm. Shelby touched them with a trembling awestruck finger, her breathing uneven. Never had she been kissed like that. Speechless, she could only stare at Billy. Their eyes locked as they breathed in unison, her cheeks coloring under the heat of his gaze.

"I guess one of us has to say something eventually." Billy's eyes danced. He looked happy, and something else Shelby couldn't quite pick, all she knew was it made her heart beat faster. "I'm wondering why it took me so darn long to kiss you after that."

Her eyes widened. *Did that mean he'd felt it in his very soul the way she had?* "Um, did you want to?" Shelby nibbled at her bottom lip, uncomfortable at how vulnerable she felt. "Kiss me, I mean."

"Even when I didn't know what to do with you, I knew I wanted to kiss you." Billy looked up at her from the corner of his eye. "It drove me crazy."

"Oh." Shelby knew she probably looked like a love-struck calf, but the idea that the gorgeous, accomplished William Irvine had been wanting to kiss her for the longest time just didn't seem real to her. "Um." She spied the toolbox. "I better get these packed up."

She picked up a spanner. Surprised, she stared at him when he removed it firmly from her hand. "I can pack up, Shelby. It's the least I can do since you're the reason I get to have a shower." Shelby's mind veered sharply to Billy, wet in a shower. Maybe she was the one who needed one—a cold one!

"Well, if you're sure. I reckon I might go for a walk and explore the island." Maybe that would burn some of the nervous energy firing through her veins.

Rubbing her hands on her back pockets, she left him to it. Finding a boardwalk that hugged the edge of the tree line, she wound her way through coconut groves and bunches of banana trees. Some of the brightly colored flowers she could identify like the hibiscus and the frangipanis, but others, like the garish orange spires, she had as much clue to what they were as to how to describe the kiss she'd just had with Billy. Again, her fingers found their way of their own free will to delicately trace where his lips had touched hers. After that kiss, she couldn't imagine ever being kissed by another. Shelby shivered just thinking about the possibility of more delicious moments spent in Billy's arms.

Balmy salt air danced across her skin as she rounded the corner and found herself on a headland. She skidded to a halt when she saw Maura with something clasped to her chest, staring dejectedly out across the sparkling azure waters. Her misery seemed at odds with the awe-inspiring location.

"I'm sorry, I didn't know you were here. I didn't mean to intrude."

Maura's smile did little to hide her red-rimmed eyes. "I should be getting back." She moved to slip whatever was in her hands into her pocket.

Shelby caught a glimpse of what looked to be an old photograph. "My mom always says it lessens the load if you share it. I'm a pretty good listener."

Maura hesitated before opening her hand. With a tender finger she traced something on the photo before looking up at Shelby and, with a sadness shadowing her eyes, handed it to her. Shelby looked at it curiously, feeling honored that she'd been trusted to hold the treasured memory. A younger version of Maura stood on a sandy beach, her hair tossed by the wind. In her arms, a young boy—no more than two years old—stared adoringly up at her as she twirled him about.

"Is this your son?"

"Yes." Maura retrieved the photo from Shelby like it had pained her to be parted from it for even that short period of time and stashed it safely back into her pocket.

"Do you get to see him much?' Shelby wanted to kick herself for being obtuse. Obviously, Maura didn't, otherwise she wouldn't be crying over an old photograph. Horrified, she prayed he wasn't dead.

"I get to see him more than I have a right to. But still, I miss him every day." There was a haunted, lost quality in the way she looked at Shelby. An intense pain that bordered on physical. "If you'll excuse me, I really do need to get back to work."

Not waiting for a reply, Maura hurried away. Shelby could only watch the older woman leave, her heart breaking for an untold story she could only guess at. Sighing, she found a spot on the rocks and gazed pensively out at the Pacific. It seemed to be the spot for it.

CHAPTER 15

*H*e stared at the flashing phone as it rang. Idly, he wondered when the last time he'd even thought about work was. Hours? Days? It was oddly liberating to realize he'd been perfectly happy without micromanaging his time in the pursuit of making money. Smiling, William reached for the phone. Misty would think he had too much sun if he admitted it to her.

"Hello, my gorgeous business partner."

"You sound disgustingly upbeat," Misty greeted him. "Are you living like Robinson Crusoe on your new island?"

William snorted at the image of him in palm frond woven pants, talking to her on a phone made of two coconut shells tied together with some twine. The thought of Shelby better utilizing those coconuts as part of his fantasy island wardrobe was much more appealing. "No, it has all the modern amenities—well, now that Shelby's made it so I can have a shower again. Why?"

"Do I even want to know why Shelby is the gatekeeper to showering? Actually, don't bother answering that. You haven't been checking your emails. Are you sick?"

"No, I don't think I've ever felt better." William began to feel guilty at having let his commitments slide. "I assumed Dana would take care of things."

"She has, but I was too impatient to not keep checking the figures."

It suddenly dawned on William that Misty was calling him from her honeymoon. "Hang on, why are you calling me about business? Why aren't you off annoying your husband?"

"Oh, pish, you sound just like him. Believe me, he's getting more attention than he knows how to handle. Anyway, we leave for home tomorrow. This was only a micro-honeymoon. We'll have the real one later, and trust me, he won't have anything to complain about then."

William's mind shivered away from that disturbing visual. "More than I need to know, Misty. Are you going to tell me why you're calling, or do I need to go check my email?"

"I'm getting there. You're the one who's distracting me by asking personal questions. Mr Onissios called. He can't keep up with all the orders for the lotus silk collection. He believes it's going to be an extremely profitable textile. But there's more." She paused dramatically. "Everyone's trying to find out who Shelby is. You'd better warn her that she isn't going to be an unknown when she comes home. The gal's famous."

Conflicting emotions buffeted William. He'd never known it was possible to experience the warm glow of pride whilst the cold hand of uncertainty twisted itself in his belly. "I'm not sure Shelby's going to be stoked," he finally managed to utter.

"Well, be gentle when you tell her, and make sure she understands how big of a deal this is for her. It's quite liter-ally life-changing."

As he hung up, the realization hit him that he'd finally found a sense of peace with himself—thanks to Shelby—and now, ironically, he irrevocably understood what Misty had tried to tell him months ago. Shelby really was too good for him, but not if he became a man worthy of her. William found a perverse pleasure in the idea. He'd spent his life shaping himself into his personal vision of success, and now he was going to scrape it back to the bone and expose the man he could be—all in the name of love. Chuckling at how hard he'd fallen without realizing it, he went in search of his cowgirl.

Turns out what he was really in search of was a mermaid. Sitting perched on her rock, long sandy blonde hair whipping about her face, she stared pensively out to sea like her soul yearned to be reunited with her saltwater heart. William shook his head at the nonsense. Since when had he got so fantastical in his musings?

"I'm pretty sure it's illegal to be unhappy on an island. Maybe you need another kiss. Or is that what's making you so glum?"

Color flared to life on her tanned cheeks. *Would he ever get tired of teasing her just to see her reaction?* "No, I was just thinking about something." Her eyes widened in denial before dropping behind the cover of her thick, dark eyelashes.

His gaze roamed her face, searching for her inner thoughts. "I'm a bit disappointed it's not the kiss. I haven't been able to think about anything else since."

Shelby's eyes grew large and watery as she raised her gaze to stare up at him. "Really?"

Billy couldn't resist leaning forward until his lips were level with her ear. "With every breath I've taken." Smug male satisfaction filled him at the delicate shiver that trembled through her. Feeling pleased with himself, he sat back and dribbled some water from the bottle he carried onto her foot.

She jerked back, eyes wide in shock. "What was that for?"

"Just checking."

"That I didn't melt?"

"That you didn't turn into a mermaid. Maybe it has to be saltwater. Wait here and I'll go get some." William made a show of standing up, ready to head to the shore.

Shelby looked at him like he'd lost his mind—and maybe he had—but gosh if it didn't feel amazing to play a little. "Maybe you should start wearing a hat when you're out in the sun."

"Maybe." He sat down again. "Now, are you going to tell me why you're sitting here looking like your heart's breaking?"

"I just saw Maura and she was really upset. I think maybe she has a bit of a sad past. What do you know about her?"

"Nothing much really. She comes with good references and has a solid work history. She isn't married and has no dependents listed, which makes her perfect to look after my island for me." He squinted at Shelby. *Maybe the hat was a good idea.* "You probably know as much about her as I do."

"Well, I know she has a son," Shelby offered, peering hard at him. "I guess he'd be grown now."

"Well, grown children don't really bother me too much. It's the little ones who need constant care that would be an issue with her living out here." A rumble of his stomach interrupted him. All this fresh air had really given him an appetite. "I think that's my cue to say it's dinner," he said, holding his hand out to her.

Shelby nodded, accepting the proffered hand, a faraway look in her eye as they made their way back to the villa. *Hopefully she's thinking about that kiss.*

William smiled at Maura in greeting as they made their way to the pavilion that served as an eating area. *Seriously, buying this island was the best thing he'd ever done. That, and buying a car that broke down. So, this was what feeling genuinely happy felt like. Addictive.* Shelby pulled her hand from his.

Confused, he turned back to find out what had happened. William frowned when he found her pale-faced and staring at Maura in shock. *Surely she wasn't embarrassed to show affection in front of the caretaker, was she?*

Shelby's wide-eyed gaze darted between him and the chalky-faced Maura. "I can't believe I didn't see it before. It was right in front of me, and you can tell when you know to look for it."

William frowned, looking between the two of them, the tension palpable. "Is someone going to let me in on the secret?"

It was as though he hadn't spoken, the two women wholly consumed by the other. "I'm right, aren't I?" Shelby asked, her tone baffling in its gentleness. William watched as Maura, nostrils flared, shook her head in denial, her eyes shimmering as if on the point of tears. "Billy, you look like her."

"Please, no," Maura whispered, agony in every line on her face.

Shelby gazed at Maura with an infinite tenderness. "He deserves to know." Half in anticipation, half in dread, William watched Shelby turn to him. "What do you remember about your mother?"

"There's nothing to remember. All I know is she deserves to end up in the same place as the man she left me with." His voice hardened ruthlessly, ignoring the quickly smothered cry from Maura. "She didn't care about me. She knew what he was like and she still left me there, only worrying about herself." Tears were now streaming down the older woman's face.

"BILLY," Shelby said in an odd, but gentle voice. "Maura's your mother."

Struck by wave after wave of disgust, rage and betrayal from her words, it felt almost like an out-of-body experience. A tormented Maura, fearful and hopeful at the same time and seemed to be on the verge of vomiting, stood rooted to the spot. Shelby gazed nervously between them, waiting for an eruption. And himself—he could see his body standing there, blank-faced, a spectator to the bombshell that had been thrust into their midst. And then, with a jerk, he was back in his body and, with quick strides, had grabbed Maura roughly by her shoulders.

"Is it true?" A quiet menace in his voice.

Maura nodded mutely. Her eyes pleading with him where her voice could not.

William thrust her away from him in disgust. "Did you take this job to try to extort money from me? To spy on me? Blackmail? I can tell you now that better people than you have tried and failed."

"William, I—" Maura finally found her voice, but he was too filled with blind rage to let her finish.

"I don't want to hear anything that comes from your lying mouth. You pack your things and make sure I never see you again."

"Billy." He brushed Shelby's restraining hand from his arm. Not trusting himself with violence swirling through his veins, he stormed away from the trauma of his past made real in the flesh.

Sometimes he could still hear his father's mocking voice, feel the blows that had landed on his broken body. That evil wore a face he knew. But over the years, the mother who had abandoned him, she'd been made into a monster too. Her evil face a mass of decaying flesh. Not the warmly smiling woman who'd greeted them on the dock. How was her corruption not showing?

"Billy?" Shelby tentatively called from the shadows. "I'm sorry. I should've given you time, maybe softened it a bit."

William realized that he'd ended up on the mermaid rocks of earlier that day. Now it felt more like sea monsters were attacking his soul, sucking him down into the undertow. "How long have you known?"

"I only just pieced it all together then. I found her crying this afternoon"—Shelby sat heavily down on a rock—"right here. I know it's a shock."

"I don't want to talk about it," he ground out, rancor sharpening his voice.

"She's your mom."

"You've made that perfectly clear," he replied sharply.

"But don't you want to hear her side of things?"

He whirled to stare at her, hot anger burning through him. "Why would I want to do that? She lied to us—to me. Obviously to get close enough to get money." William's breath burned in his throat. "She's no mother to me. She's been dead to me a long time and there's no reason for that to change now."

Soft hands turned his rage-scalded gaze to hers. "Billy, I think you need to talk to her. Not for her, but for you, the little boy you were, for him to finally get closure on why. Then if you decide to never see her again, you can move on with your life. But whatever you decide to do, I'm right here beside you. Because"—she swallowed, her eyes shining a question up into his—"I love you."

A bucket of icy cold water doused the flames of his rampaging emotions as he stared back at her. Hurt, so intense it felt like physical pain, stabbed William. He was that little boy again, alone with a monster and no one to save him. Deep sobs racked at his insides, forcing their way out of him as hot tears blinded him. His father was right. He was a sissy.

Turning away before Shelby could in disgust at his weakness, he wiped angrily at the tears. And then those wonderfully tender hands were there again, caressing the sadness from his face before covering every inch of it in butterfly soft kisses. William could only gaze at her in amazement that she wasn't repulsed by him with all his unmanliness exposed.

He wrapped an arm around her, and she snuggled in close to his side, her arm snaking around the small of his back. William breathed in deeply, drawing on the comfort of her nearness. She loved him? She'd seen him like this and she still loved him? Silently locked together, he listened to the beat of his pulverized heart and knew it was no longer his. It was all hers.

CHAPTER 16

*T*he fan swirled lazily, dark shadows against the ceiling. Throwing back his covers in disgust, William pushed himself off the bed. It made no sense staying in bed when sleep was so clearly going to evade him. On bare feet, he padded from his room in search of a glass of milk—or something stronger.

The light from the kitchen shone down the covered pathway, almost like a beacon. Displeased, he pursed his lips at the waste of energy. He would have to make sure the new caretaker was more stringent than the last on conserving the resources available on the island.

Speak of the devil. Maura, red-eyed, guiltily rose from the table when he entered. Her cheeks were damp with tears. William was irked by the pain that poked at him when he saw her. Angrily, he glared at her. How dare she make him feel like she was the wounded party in this fiasco he called his life!

"I thought I'd made myself clear I never wanted to see you again." His caustic tone made her already pale cheeks turn ashen under her tears.

Maura's expression was one of mute regret. "I'm sorry. I didn't think anyone would still be up. I'll go back to my room," she said in a low tormented voice.

"Shelby says I should hear what you have to say. Apparently, it will make all the terrible things that happened to me go away." She flinched under his lashing hatred. "So, tell me then. What did I do to you? Because I can't think of anything that justified the hell you left me in." William swallowed down the bile that rose in his throat. "Do you know that I actually thought it was normal to be locked in an airless, dark cupboard every night? That that's just what families did?"

Soundless sobs shook her frame as though physical pain racked her body. "I didn't leave you. You were my baby." Maura heaved in a shuddering breath. "I'm so sorry I couldn't find you."

It was like William had lost feeling in his body. The only awareness he had was the tormented woman in front of him, his mother. "What do you mean? You left me."

"No, I didn't." Her eyes pleaded with him to believe her. "I took you and I ran as far and fast as I could. He told me he'd kill me if I took you away, but I didn't care. Don't you remember?"

"No, you left me with him. You didn't care about me and you left me like I was trash." William could only repeat the rhetoric he'd had drummed into him his entire life.

"No, I didn't. I started making a new life for us. It wasn't much, but we were safe and happy, and then one day I went to pick you up from Mrs Gunnery's. She was the elderly neighbor who used to look after you when I had to work—I had three jobs to make ends meet. She met me at the door, and I still remember the smell of the cookies baking as she wiped her hands on her apron and said your father had picked you up. That it had all been arranged and I must have forgotten to tell her. She even tsked at me to not let it happen again." Maura sunk back down into her chair as if her legs could no longer support her body. "I drove through the night to get to where your father used to live and when I got there, people I didn't know told me they owned the house now. I tried everything to find you. When I finally raised enough money, I hired a PI, but even he couldn't find you. It was like you had just disappeared. Do you know what that was like? Every birthday—every Christmas—I wrapped presents for you. I thought about you on the day you would have graduated and wondered at the man you'd become without me. I never stopped loving you."

William hated how much he desperately wanted to believe his mother's story. Yet still, he wrapped the mantle of his anger about him. "That doesn't quite explain how you ended up on my island. You seem to have landed on your feet for someone so grief-stricken."

She gave him a sad, watery little smile. "Life goes on, even when you don't want it to. I'd been raised near the sea, and when I had nothing left to live for, it called to me. I started working on yachts. First small, and then gradually on the superyachts of the rich and famous, and I sailed the oceans for years, never wanting to stay in the one place for too long. I never stopped looking for you. And last year, one of the owners of the yacht gave the details of an investigator they'd used in a divorce and I used all of my savings to hire him. He discovered you were my son, but then I saw you were a billionaire and I knew you wouldn't want me for a mom. Later I read an article that you'd bought this island, and on the same day the agency I got jobs from contacted me about this job and I applied. It just seemed like fate was trying to bring us together and I surrendered to it. I was never going to tell you who I was. I just wanted to see the sort of man you'd grown into, to be near you. That's all."

William was assailed by a terrible sense of bitterness. It suddenly made sense to him. "You want money from me." It wasn't a question, but a cold statement of fact.

Maura recoiled, hurt blanching her features. Hurt and longing lay naked in her eyes. "No! I don't want money. You're the one who rose above a horrendous situation. I—" She swallowed, pressing her lips together, appearing to gather herself. "I failed you when I didn't protect you. I've spent a lifetime going over that day, wondering how he found us. But he did. I just want you to be happy and I think you are. That's enough for me." She stood, holding the table for support. "I'll go back to my room." Maura paused, pride shining from her tear-stained face. "I'm proud of you, my son, and I love you. You might not want to hear that right now, but I do." Shoulders stooped, she walked from the room, disappearing in the dark outside.

William stood frozen to the spot. His mind heaving under the overload of conflicting thoughts and emotions, threatening to snap. Getting control of his limbs, he stalked to the counter and snatched a bottle of liquor. He wasn't even sure what it was, but anything would do as long as it quietened his mind. Gulping it down, he sunk into a chair, realizing too late that it was the one his mother had sat in. William could still feel the warmth of her body. A sensation of intense sickness and wretchedness swept over him. Covering his face with trembling hands, he gave vent to his agony.

"Billy?" Shelby could only just make out the shape of a body on the bed as she poked her head through his bedroom door. "Billy, are you awake?"

"No."

Closing the door quietly behind her, she tiptoed closer. "Are you okay?"

"I was till someone woke me up," he grumbled at her. She wasn't even sure he'd opened his eyes.

"I was just wondering, um, it's really beautiful here, and maybe I should call Misty and tell her we're staying for another few days."

"You want to stay?"

"Yeah." She sat down on the edge of the bed, twisting the edge of the sheet around it. "That is, if you want to?"

"Shelby, I can't think of anywhere else I'd rather be than in paradise with you." In the dim light, she could see the gleam of his eye. *Good, he wasn't pretending to be asleep anymore.*

"In that case, maybe we should tell Maura to stop packing. Won't we need her here, at least until a replacement can come?" Shelby held her breath, unsure if Billy was going to explode or simply turn his back on her. Both would be equally bad.

"I talked to her last night."

Shelby's mouth dropped opened. "And?"

"She told me some things. I'm not sure how I feel about them," he said in a tense, clipped voice that forbade any further questions.

She had never been any good at following directions. "Is she staying?"

"I haven't decided yet." Billy rolled onto his side, propping himself up on his elbow. "If I'm to believe her, she never abandoned me. In fact, she claims she spent my whole life trying to find me."

Shelby stared at him. This was a plot twist she hadn't seen coming and wasn't entirely sure what to say. "Do you believe her?"

"That's the thing. I don't know. I worked so hard because

I thought that, if I was rich, I'd be somebody—that I'd proved I was worth something to somebody, even if it was just me. And now I find out I was always worth something to someone and she just couldn't find me. My whole life is based on a lie." He raised tormented eyes to hers. "In Paris you asked me if I knew who I was without all the fame and money, and now I know the answer. I'm Maura's son."

CHAPTER 17

*H*e could hear the muted movements inside the room. "I'd like you to have this, Shelby," William heard his mother say. He hadn't quite anticipated Shelby being in there, maybe he should come back another time.

"It's gorgeous, Maura. I'm usually a Stetson or baseball cap kinda gal, but this is perfect for island living." There were more rustling noises inside. He could picture the two women hugging it out. Somehow it was oddly okay with him.

William tentatively knocked. His mouth trembled when Shelby answered the door. Somehow seeing her gently encouraging smile took all the wind out of his sails. "I love you, Billy, and no matter what happens here, I still will." Shelby laid a soft kiss on his lips before, with a final smile, she walked past him and out of the room.

"I know I don't have the right, but if you don't tell that girl how you really feel, you're a fool." Maura didn't look up from where she was folding clothes on her bed in preparation for packing. "She's special, and she sure as heck isn't with you for the money. You could lose it all tomorrow and she'd be happy to share some fries as long as it was with you."

Resentment warred with surprise at her insight. "What makes you think I haven't?"

Maura's keen observant eyes stared him down. "Because she doesn't have the look of someone who knows that the man she loves loves her back. You might have told her you care, but you haven't opened your heart to her."

"And who's fault would it be that I'm not very good at expressing emotions?" William felt uncomfortable that maybe she'd spoken the truth. "I've never said those words to anyone I've dated before, and Shelby and I, well, it's complicated. We aren't even actually dating." He shifted uncomfortably. Why was he spilling his guts to this woman he barely knew? Mother or not.

"Love is only as complicated as you want to make it. Don't miss out on something with Shelby because of me and your father."

Something clicked in his mind. The harder he tried to ignore the truth, the more it persisted. "Look, Maura, I don't really know you, and I can't make any promises. There's still a lot I need to process about you and what you told me. I can't even guess how much it's going to cost me in therapy, but maybe we should at least get to know each other before I decide if I want you in my life or not."

Her eyes shimmered as she gazed at him in wonderous amazement. "I'd like that."

Slowly, as though terrified that he would run away if she moved too quickly, she reached her hand out until it touched his. The loving touch of a mother he'd thought long forsaken shook him to his very core. Hesitantly, he laid his hand over hers. *Baby steps.*

"HEY, MOM."

"Shelby, what's the island like? Tell me all about it," Shelby's mother excitedly asked.

"Um, well, I think it might be as close as you can get to the Garden of Eden in this lifetime. It's beautiful. It's finer than frog fur, and that's a fact." Emotion choked her at the thought that this would all be over soon. "It's something I never imagined existed." Tears burned, threatening to break free. Really, she was being dumber than a barrel of hair.

"What's wrong, Shelby?"

"Nothing, Mom."

"Shelby Erikson, I've known you since before you were born. Now, something is obviously up. You can either wallow in it alone or talk about it. Remember, a problem shared is a problem halved."

Shelby smiled. She never had been able to fool her mom. "I don't even know where to begin."

"At the beginning is as good a place as any."

"Billy and I have been getting closer. Like, really close, Mom." *Geeze, that didn't even half cover how it felt.*

"But?" her mother prompted

"So much has happened—not just with the fashion show or since we've come to the island—I could write a novel about it. But I told him I loved him." Shelby still couldn't quite believe she'd actually said it to him. It wasn't like she'd expected him to come straight back and say it to her. The poor man had a lot on his plate.

"Shelby, I'm so happy for you. I know Logan will be so excited to have another man sitting around the table at Christmas."

Shelby could only imagine what Logan would have to say. "Mom, you're getting a little ahead of yourself. I said I loved him, but he hasn't said anything about loving me." She sniffled. "And now we're about to leave this island and it'll all be over." The dam holding back her tears broke. "I don't want it to be over with Billy."

"Then you need to talk to Billy. A lot of men find it hard to express their emotions—like your father, for example. Doesn't mean he doesn't feel deep, he just ain't always got the words for them."

Her mother's words soothed the fear from her heart. Maybe all hope wasn't lost after all. "Thanks, Mom, I miss you."

"I miss you too, but you'll be home soon enough, and you can tell me all about your adventures over a jug of sweet tea."

Shelby laughed through her tears. "I think it'll take more than one jug." It was funny how a little perspective could make the future seem a little less bleak. Maybe there was hope for her and Billy after all.

CHAPTER 18

*L*ife was to be lived in the fast lane. Pulsing lights and culture. At least, that's what William used to think. Standing at the gateway to the villa, he felt a rising wave of tension, the contentment that had cocooned him evaporating as surely as water in the desert.

Maura gave him a little smile, her eyes shadowed with uncertainty. "I guess this is goodbye."

"No, it's a till I see you again," he said firmly. "I'm still arranging for another caretaker, but you're more than welcome to stay on as my guest." He swallowed. "Or maybe come to New York from time to time."

Her eyes shimmered with unshed tears. "I like the sound of that." She turned at Shelby's approaching footsteps. "It was a pleasure to meet you."

The cowgirl wrapped her in a fierce embrace. "Don't be a stranger, Maura. I'm sure my mom would love to meet you."

Maura sniffled. "I think I'd like to meet her, too, if her daughter is anything to go by."

The realization struck William that the two women

standing in front of him were well on their way to becoming friends. He found the thought oddly satisfying. Before he could change his mind, he reached out for his mother and hugged her before pulling back. "You have my number?"

Maura stared at him like she'd just won the lotto. "Yes."

Shelby smiled brilliantly at him as she spoke. "And you gave her your email, too."

He shifted his weight whimsically, not wanting to leave this special place, but nonetheless eager to rejoin the real world as well. "Well then, we better get going." William looked to Shelby for agreement. He thought she seemed a little sad. Maybe this island held as special a place in her heart as his.

The last thing he saw as the boat pulled away was Maura getting smaller and smaller in the distance, waving as though she never expected to see them again. He vowed that she would.

"What city is that down there?" Shelby pressed her nose to the airplane window.

Could she look anymore adorable? "Baltimore."

Her brows scrunched as she stared at him in uncertainty. "Baltimore Baltimore?" The last one ended in a little squeak.

"As far as I know, there's only one." William chuckled. "But I could be wrong. I was once before."

"What?"

"Wrong. I was wrong when I was in college. I didn't really like it, so I decided to never do it again."

Shelby captured his eyes with her long-suffering gaze. "Not you being wrong. Baltimore. Why are we flying over Baltimore?"

He really was enjoying teasing her too much, but dang if it wasn't fun. "Because Baltimore is on the way to New York."

"New York?" she squeaked in repeat.

"Oh"—he slapped his forehead—"I must've forgotten to tell you that we're detouring to New York for a night and then on to Texas in the morning."

Her eyes narrowed. "Why?"

"My, you're full of questions today, aren't you?"

"Yes, especially when you spring surprises on me like this. Billy, why are we going to New York first instead of straight to Texas?" She skewered him with a steely look. "And don't try to be cute this time."

He gazed at her in feigned innocence, holding his hand over his heart. "You wound me, Shelby, you really do. I'm always cute."

"Billy, I swear to God, if you don't start talking soon, I'm going to lose my last nerve." *She was even cuter when she was getting cranky.*

"Because I want to show you something, that's why. Trust me."

She sucked on the inside of her cheek, mulling it over. "Fine. But only if you stop being"—she gestured at him—"like this. I'm not sure I like this happy Billy as much as the coldly-driven one."

"Deal." He leaned back comfortably in his seat. "Now, would you like to hear the story about the one time I was wrong in my life?"

"No!"

"It was a rainy day in November—"

"Stop it!"

William turned and stared out the window to hide the smile spreading across his face. Maybe the island or Paris weren't the only places he could feel that happy. Maybe it was as long as he was with Shelby.

～

SHELBY COULD ONLY STARE in open-mouthed wonder at the spectacle in front of her. Bouncing from foot to foot, her head swiveled about as she tried to take it all in. It felt like her insides were vibrating. Everywhere there were neon lights, colors, movement. She paused a moment in her restless movements. But it also seemed artless and congested. Times Square was like everything good and bad about New York City had somehow been concentrated into this one place.

She tugged at the hem of her dress that had ridden up. *Soon it'll be back to jeans and overalls.* Shelby stole a glance at Billy who was waiting patiently while she took it all in. Her heart spasmed painfully. *Soon he won't be around.*

He smiled broadly at her. Although he'd returned to his usual immaculate attire—the one she'd identified with him for so long—somehow, he seemed more relaxed. Like he'd undone a top button or missed a manicure. Shelby thought it was bittersweet that he wore the clothes he'd had before he'd left, but somehow the experiences they'd shared together had left a mark on him. She knew it had on her.

"If you're done staring at the perfection that is moi, shall we walk a bit?" The warmth of Billy's voice was echoed in his eyes as he held out his hand. "What I want to show you is only a little bit further, I promise."

Shelby's fingers tingled when they touched his, a pleasant friction between their palms. "It must be crazy here on New Year's Eve."

"You have no idea. Have I told you how beautiful you look in that dress?"

"Only like a million times." She tugged at the hem again.

"But you're looking forward to getting back to normal?"

"A little." *But not all of me.*

His gaze traveled the length of her body. "For what it's worth, you've converted me."

Shelby lowered her gaze in confusion. "Converted you to what?"

"A while ago, some might have called me a snob." She stared guilelessly back at him before the corners of his mouth softened. "And they would have been right. You look beautiful in that dress, but I think I prefer the Shelby in jeans or, lately, in kaftans." With a gentle pressure he pulled her to a halt. "But we also have Shelby on the side of a building." Incredulously, she raised her gaze to take in the humungous digital billboard. A billboard with her on it. Shelby could only stare at him, stunned disbelief robbing her of words. Eyes twinkling mischievously, Billy looked between the billboard and her. "Didn't we tell you about this?"

"No," she breathed.

"Excuse me, mate?" a tourist with an Aussie twang interrupted. "Is that your mug up there?" He jabbed a thumb in the direction of the billboard.

"It most certainly is," Billy answered for her, grinning smugly. "Would you like a picture with her in front of it?"

"That'd be ripper."

Shelby could only move in a dreamlike trance as she posed with first the Australian and then a steady stream of others as they were swarmed.

At last, when her aching cheeks felt like they couldn't take anymore, Billy graciously declined more requests and wrapped an arm snuggly about her. "It looks like you're famous."

There was a slightly hysterical edge to the giggle that escaped her. "I'm not sure how I feel about that."

"I think it was naïve for either of us to think things

wouldn't change, that we could just go back to how things were before."

Shelby's heart began to beat so loudly she was amazed he didn't feel it beating against him. "Excuse me, Shelby?" She didn't recognize the voice, but she could quite happily throttle whoever it was for interrupting him.

She peered past Billy to see a tall, skinny girl. She looked vaguely familiar in a beautiful generic way. "Yes?"

She felt Billy's arm tense slightly, his eyes narrowed as he stared at the woman. "Aren't you one of Annika's friends?"

The model's eyes darted away guiltily, her mouth scrunching unattractively. "Yeah, I know Annika."

"Did you come out to see Shelby's billboard?" he pressed.

"Ah, no. Actually, I came out to see mine." She pointed at something in the distance.

All Shelby could see was something advertising dog food. She squinted. "The one with the dog?"

"No, below it," the model muttered sheepishly.

Shelby peered and noticed a billboard being towed by a scooter. Her eyes widened as she took in the model lounging in a bed of toilet paper, a caption proclaiming it soft as silk. "Is that you?"

Billy threw his head back and laughed uproariously, the rumble vibrating through him. "Have you considered other careers? Because it seems like modeling has really gone down the toilet for you."

"Billy!" Shelby gave him a light warning tap on the arm.

"Oh, I'm not finished yet." There was a fierce gleam in his eyes as he took in the other woman. "Seriously, I'd start thinking about what you're going to do once modeling is over for you because it doesn't seem like it's going to last very much longer, and Lord knows you don't have much of a personality to fall back on. Newsflash, people don't like mean girls, and looks fade."

With a hurt huff, the model stomped away, ignoring Shelby's mocking wave of farewell. She knew she should feel bad for the telling off the other woman had just been on the receiving end of, but she wasn't a hypocrite. She'd thoroughly deserved it and Shelby had enjoyed every moment. She burrowed an arm around the inside of Billy's jacket.

"So, do you think we can get a slice of New York pizza now?"

He kissed the top of her head. "I think I can arrange that."

Holding her happiness closely to her heart, Shelby lifted her chin. She was determined to live tonight without sorrow. It would come soon enough.

"ARE YOU READY? I mean if we're late, I'm pretty sure the pilot will still wait for us."

Shelby plastered on a smile as she raised her eyes only to take in Billy's attire. It was a good thing she was sitting down. "What on God's green earth are you wearing?"

He gave a slow pivot, daring her to take it all in. And take it in she did. Shelby had thought Billy was the hottest man she'd ever seen the moment she'd laid eyes on him at Evelyn and Colt's wedding. She'd seen him in suits and slacks and even swim trunks, but never in the time they'd been together had she seen him in jeans. The man had a backside that, clad in denim, could make the angels sigh. Blinking, she stared down at his feet.

"Are those boots?"

"Yep." He lifted the leg of his jeans proudly. "Figured if I was going to Texas, I might as well stop resisting and look the part, darlin'." He gave his best impression of a Texan drawl, touching the brim of an imaginary Stetson.

Shelby swallowed, finding herself suddenly parched. His

words penetrated the delightful warmth that had flooded her body and apparently taken all the blood from her brain. "Sorry, did you just say you're coming to Texas, too?"

"Of course." There was a heat in the way he looked at her that belied the lightness of his words. "Did you think I would let you go without me?"

"But you don't like Texas!" she protested, feeling utterly off balance. Shelby had been fully prepared to wallow in self-pity at the pain of star-crossed unrequited love for the entire flight home, followed by ice-cream and watching *The Golden Girls* when she got there.

"But I like what they have in Texas."

"What?"

His gaze was as soft as a caress. "You."

~

You.

Shelby turned that softly spoken word over and over in her mind on the flight home. Billy had said it as intimately as a lover. Just thinking about it brought a burst of heat to her cheeks. *Seriously, Shelby, you need to get a grip. You're making a mountain out of a molehill! Think about something else.*

"Um, Billy, whatever happened to that car you drove down to Texas last time in?"

He blinked at her, obviously not expecting that particular line of questioning. A slow smile spread across his gorgeous mouth, lighting up his face. "You know, I really don't know." He rubbed at his chin, a rueful twinkle in his eyes. "Now you've got me curious. I'll have to ask Dana."

"Are you just dropping me off in Texas, or do you have plans?" Shelby twisted the loose end of her seatbelt around her finger. *Stop beating around the bush. Just ask him about us. Is there even an us?* Firmly, she removed it and clasped her fidgeting fingers tightly together.

"I'm long overdue to catch up with Misty. There's only so much nagging she can do to me over email and phone calls before they start to lose their potency. Do you mind if we swing by her ranch before I take you home? She'll get mad if we don't fill her in on all the gossip from our trip."

A cold lump of misery settled in her stomach, each breath painful. *Home. He was taking her home ... and leaving her.* Blinking, she turned back to the window, the ground below looking familiar. "Um, yeah, that's fine."

"Excellent." She could hear the rustle of paper as he returned to reading a magazine, apparently oblivious to the world of wretchedness she buried herself in.

GLUM. That's what the color of her world was going to be from now on, Shelby decided as she stared moodily down at her coffee, stirring her sugar in.

"I can't believe how successful the collection was. I mean, I hoped that Shelby would be a success, but I never imagined it would take off like this." There was an almost feverish gleam to Misty's eyes. She got like that when money was involved.

"Well, she does share my genetics, after all." Logan polished his nails on his shirt. "And you know I'm hot stuff. How much did I raise for Chora's charity again?" He winked at his wife.

"Not enough." Misty didn't even bat an eyelid at her husband's jibe.

"Mr Onissios was right. She's the perfect muse." Billy's voice washed over her, giving her pause at something hidden in its silken depths. The sharp ring of a phone interrupted the homey scene, and Billy glanced down. "Can you please excuse me? I have to take this."

Tears blurred Shelby's vision. It wasn't fair. Billy was going to be gone soon enough, and now it felt like whoever was on the other end of that call was eating into their time together. It wasn't fair, darn it!

"And William found his mother," Misty marveled. "And on his own island, of all places."

"Yeah, Maura's really nice." She was being selfish. If Maura could let her son leave after she'd only just rediscovered him, the least she could do is stop sulking. *Easier said than done.*

"How about we grab that pitcher of sweet tea in the refrigerator and go get us gals some fresh air on the patio?" Misty's hand was gentle when she laid it over Shelby's. *Why did it just make her want to cry more?* She nodded and followed her sister-in-law outside. It was a glorious afternoon, a hint of rain in the air, the sun sending bright beams of golden light spilling through the clouds. A low purring rumble rolling down the gravel drive drew her attention away from her nature appraisal.

In the distance, she could make out a low-slung convertible. Shielding her eyes, she stared incredulously as it came into view, all generous, sweeping curves, the royal blue gleaming as exquisitely as a sapphire in a rich lady's ring. A familiar dark-haired man, now tousled, sat grinning behind the steering wheel of her dream car.

"Is that a—" Shelby didn't dare utter the name, fearful it would vanish like a dream she would wake up from.

"That depends on what you think it is." Billy smirked at her, stepping out. "You're one hard lady to shop for. Any other woman who I wanted to show I loved—and there hasn't been any, so I was in unchartered territory—but I imagine I would have purchased her an insanely huge diamond and she would've been happy. But you—" He wagged his finger at her. "No, for you, I had to get this, hang on a second." Billy made a show of fishing in his pocket, pulled out a piece of paper and began to read from it. "For you, I had to get a 1966 CSX 3015 Shelby Cobra, which I'm led to believe there were only two ever made. And this particular super-snake cobra was Carrol Shelby's personal one. You have no idea how much it cost to get its previous owner to part with it." Concern flickered across his face. "Are you okay, Shelby?"

She wasn't sure what she was feeling. Hot and cold at the same time. Like she wanted to laugh and cry. Like her heart was going to beat out of her chest.

Billy walked closer and took her hands in his. "Maybe I should seize the opportunity while you're speechless." He drew in a deep breath. "This car was the only way I could think of to tell you how much I love you. Shelby, I love you with grease under your nails and smudges on your chin, and if it means I'm going to have to get my hands dirty once in a while to keep you happy, then you're worth it to me." He pressed the keys into her hand.

Shelby stood frozen, and yet all her senses leapt to life as he gathered her in his arms and held her snugly. The kiss he pressed to her lips was like a soldering iron joining metal, searing their two souls together. Even when he finally drew back, it was as though he'd left a part of him behind, forever with her.

"Did I mention I love you?"

Shelby blinked back tears that threatened. "Only, like, a billion times. Which works out pretty well, since I love you at least that much too."

Billy pulled her back to him and squeezed her like his life depended on it. Only then did she realize he was shaking. "Thank the Lord. I didn't have a backup plan if you told me you'd changed your mind. Maybe just drive off into the sunset." He kissed the top of her head where it was nestled into the hollow of his shoulder. "Do you have any idea how hard it was to find a car like this? There are lots of old rust buckets, but showroom floor condition is hard."

"I can imagine. But if you'd gotten me a rust bucket, I wouldn't have minded it. I like restoring them, taking old treasures and making them shine again."

"In that case"—he snatched the keys from her fingers —"I'll take this one back and get you something else."

Shelby darted forward and hastily retrieved them. "Don't you dare! And while we're at it, promise me you'll never drive it again. You don't have the best track record with cars."

"Ouch." He assumed a wounded expression. "Which reminds me, Dana says that my car has been sitting at the workshop for a couple of months waiting for me to pick it up." Shelby could only stare at him in amazement. What normal person did that? He gave her a smirk, obviously having had an idea. "Why don't you restore cars then? As a business?"

"Because it costs lots of money to do it right."

"Well, then it's a good thing you happen to know someone with lots of money and only one smart, beautiful cowgirl to spend it on."

"I'd like that." She felt herself coloring. "Not the spending your money on me, the restoring cars part. But where would I do it? My workshop here makes sense. It wouldn't work in Manhattan." Her voice trailed off.

"Then we should remodel the garage to fit your needs, or we can build a new one on the ranch it appears I'm about to buy." A question burned bright in his eyes.

"But what about New York? You love New York." She stammered over her choking, beating heart.

"Oh, I'm not going to fully give up New York. I'll just

travel for work and I hope you'll come with me when I do. Although I know you won't want to always leave your chickens or Poppy behind for as long as you have had to this time."

"And my worm farm."

He smiled at her so tenderly she felt her heart fill to overflowing. "Or your worm farm. I was thinking, since your parents have been looking after them all this time, we could just leave them there?"

"No!" Shelby glared at him.

"Well, then I'm thinking the ranch next door to your parent's place would be perfect. That way they can look after everything when we're away."

"That old place will need a lot of work." Shelby was already envisioning the gate in the shared boundary fence that her children could visit their grandparents through.

"We can always stay on the island until it's ready for us to move in. And believe me, it's going to take a while. Just because I'm moving to Texas doesn't mean I can live without a wine cellar or my sauna—and it definitely needs a cinema."

Shelby wasn't sure if Billy was joking or not. She suspected he wasn't, but that was okay with her. She beamed at him, still nestled in his arms. "Billy?"

"Yes?"

"Can I take my car for a drive now?"

"I'm amazed you managed to last this long."

Shelby giggled. "So am I." She wound her arms around his waist. "I love you."

Billy kissed the tip of her nose. "I love you too. Now show me what this car can really do."

Not needing to be asked again, she took her seat, smiling at the man she loved in the passenger side. She didn't know where this adventure would take them, but she knew that, with this man by her side, she had everything she'd ever want. Lovingly, she glanced at Billy, the man no longer hidden beneath his billions. As he returned her look with one that burned hotly of his own, excitement danced through her nerve endings. She put her car into gear and gunned it, flying down the gravel drive and into the sunset on the way to her very own happy ever after.

SNEAK PEEK – THE COWGIRL'S FAKE BILLIONAIRE MARRIAGE

"*Y*ou spell it C-H-O-R-A," she said to the barista for the millionth time. Today was not the day to keep her waiting for her first coffee hit of the morning. "Look, all I want is a latte and some of that chocolate cake. I don't really care what name you put on it."

Finding a spare table, Chora sat down and pulled her phone from her pocket to once again look at the dog's photo. She couldn't understand why anyone would be so cruel. But while there were people out there who treated animals despicably, her charity would be there to pick up the pieces and make sure all the critters were safe and loved. Chora glanced at her watch. Maybe she should have ordered the cake to go. She had to get to the hotel to make sure everything was going to plan for tonight's gala fundraising fashion show. It had been insane since the famous model, Shelby Erikson, had agreed to a favor for her sister-in-law. The phone had been ringing off the hook with people trying to get a ticket to what had become the hottest show in town. Misty, her long-time friend and patron, had assured her that, with what they would raise tonight, the Animals Are Forever charity wouldn't have to worry about money for a long time.

"Coral? Latte for Coral," called the barista.

Chora pushed her hair impatiently from her face as she stood, stowing the phone away. *For Pete's sake. The dude had one job to do...*

ACKNOWLEDGMENTS

A debt of gratitude to my editor Rebekah Groves for her patience with me.

Another big thanks to Megan from Designed with Grace for her cover design.

To my amazing beta readers and street team, you guys rock and I couldn't do it without you.

And finally to my fabulous alpha reader Trixie Norman, for all the late nights of reading and endless questions about your thoughts.

ALSO BY EDITH MACKENZIE

Have you read them all?

Billionaire Hearts Ranch Series

A Cowboy's Riches (Prequel)

She's broken free and is ready to fly...or ride, as the case may be...

Buy Now

The Wounded Cowboy Billionaire

He had all the money in the world—and it wasn't enough to keep his life from falling apart...

Buy Now

The Billionairess' Cowboy

He broke her heart once. She's not about to let him do it again...

Buy Now

The Billionaire's Cowgirl

They were polar opposites who thought they had it all...until they met each other...

Buy Now

The Cowgirl's Fake Billionaire Marriage

Chora's story coming soon

Buy Now

Barrels and Hearts Series

A Bull Rider's Paradise

The prequel to the Barrels and Hearts series. True love is only the beginning....of the story. Find out where it all began with Ana and Eduardo. Sometimes finding love is easy. It's keeping it that's hard.

Buy here

A Cowgirl's Dream

An Aussie cowgirl far from home. A handsome Brazilian bull rider. Can they have a rodeo love story of their dreams?

Buy Now

A Cowgirl's Heart

An Aussie cowgirl in need. Her childhood friend to the rescue. Can friendship turn into a love story?

Buy Now

A Cowgirl's Passion

One feisty cowgirl. One steadfast Brazilian bull rider. Will she see what is right in front of her?

Buy Now

A Cowgirl's Pride

An Aussie cowgirl from the wrong side of the tracks. A handsome equine vet. Can they find a way to have their happy ever after?

Buy Now

A Cowgirl's Love

A young Aussie cowgirl. A widowed rancher. Does age matter when it comes to love?

Buy Now

A Cowgirl's Movie Star

A fiery cowgirl with big dreams. A movie star far from home. When their two worlds collide, will their love be strong enough to hold them together or will they be pulled apart

Buy Now

A Cowgirl's Billionaire

A cowgirl adrift. A broken billionaire cowboy. Can he free himself from the past to be the man she needs now?

Buy Now

Cowboy Christmas Series

The Mistletoe Collection

Boots and Mistletoe

Cowboy boots, mistletoe, and a holiday do-over…

Buy Now

The Cowboy Under the Mistletoe

It'll take more than the magic of the season to help this grump find her happily ever after…

Buy Now

Mistletoe and the Billionaire's Cowgirl

He's the last man she wants this holiday season. Too bad he's exactly what she needs…

Buy Now

ABOUT THE AUTHOR

Edith MacKenzie or Eddie Mac to her friends is an author of sweet and wholesome contemporary cowboy romance. They say in literary circles to write what you know, and Eddie has certainly taken that to heart. Before embarking on a writing career, she trained horses professionally and brings that wealth of knowledge to her writing.

Now a mum to a boy and girl, as well as wife, she delights with her tales of strong cowgirls and their adventures in finding love. When not weaving the love stories of her characters, she enjoys hanging out with her family and animals, as well as reading, fishing and camping.

Just remember—once a cowgirl, always a cowgirl.

facebook.com/EddieMacAuthor

instagram.com/edith_mackenzie_author

amazon.com/Edith-MacKenzie

bookbub.com/profile/edith-mackenzie

twitter.com/edith_mackenzie

www.ingramcontent.com/pod-product-compliance
Lightning Source LLC
Chambersburg PA
CBHW032003130726
47903CB00012B/923